"Hey, Ranger,"

Hannah said, poking her tousled head into the truck to smile at him, that devastating, bright, cute-rocker-girl smile that had caught his attention the first time he'd been to Lonely Hearts Station.

His heart hit his boots.

He didn't like it when she smiled like that. There might be busted parts of his anatomy in his future!

"Listen," he said, "maybe the Mississippi riverboat isn't such a good idea for you."

"Why not?" She opened her eyes, big and innocent, and he gathered himself up to do verbal battle.

"You're too delicate. Far too innocent," he said importantly. "It sounds very dangerous to be an unchaperoned female on a boat where men will be carousing and…other things."

Her stare had a twinkle in it, and the smile she gave him almost melted his heart. "So maybe you should come with me."

RANGER'S WILD WOMAN
Tina Leonard

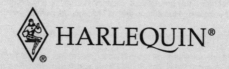

HARLEQUIN®

TORONTO • NEW YORK • LONDON
AMSTERDAM • PARIS • SYDNEY • HAMBURG
STOCKHOLM • ATHENS • TOKYO • MILAN • MADRID
PRAGUE • WARSAW • BUDAPEST • AUCKLAND

ISBN 0-373-16986-8

RANGER'S WILD WOMAN

Copyright © 2003 by Tina Leonard.

This edition published by arrangement with Harlequin Books S.A.

Visit us at www.eHarlequin.com

Printed in U.S.A.

ABOUT THE AUTHOR

Tina Leonard loves to laugh, which is one of the many reasons she loves writing Harlequin American Romance books. In another lifetime, Tina thought she would be single and an East Coast fashion buyer forever. The unexpected happened when Tina met Tim again after many years—she hadn't seen him since they'd attended school together from first through eighth grade. They married, and now Tina keeps a close eye on her school-age children's friends! Lisa and Dean keep their mother busy with soccer, gymnastics and horseback riding. They are proud of their mom's "kissy books" and eagerly help her any way they can. Tina hopes that readers will enjoy the love of family she writes about in her books. Recently a reviewer wrote, "Leonard has a wonderful sense of the ridiculous," which Tina loved so much she wants it for her epitaph. Right now, however, she's focusing on her wonderful life and writing a lot more romance!

Books by Tina Leonard

HARLEQUIN AMERICAN ROMANCE
748—COWBOY COOTCHIE-COO
758—DADDY'S LITTLE DARLINGS
771—THE MOST ELIGIBLE...DADDY
796—A MATCH MADE IN TEXAS
811—COWBOY BE MINE
829—SURPRISE! SURPRISE!
846—SPECIAL ORDER GROOM
873—HIS ARRANGED MARRIAGE
905—QUADRUPLETS ON THE DOORSTEP
977—FRISCO JOE'S FIANCÉE†
981—LAREDO'S SASSY SWEETHEART†
986—RANGER'S WILD WOMAN†

HARLEQUIN INTRIGUE
576—A MAN OF HONOR

†Cowboys by the Dozen

There are a lot of folks who keep me inspired,
and I'd like to thank them, starting with my grandmother.
Love ya, Mimi!
Lisa and Dean—Mumzie adores you!

What would I do without my cool editors
and the many wonderful folks at Harlequin
who keep me working and coherent? Thanks!

Georgia Haynes, wonderful proofreader
and brainstormer—yee-haw!

And a special thank-you to the wonderful
Scandalous Ladies: Debbie Gilbert, Maria D. Velazquez,
Ellen Kennedy, Wendy Crutcher, Debbie Jett aka dj,
Debora Hosey, Fatin Soufan and Kendra Patterson.
You gals have added so much spice and fun to my life!

Prologue

A man wants what he can't have, not always to
his betterment.
—Maverick Jefferson explaining to his
young sons why they couldn't ride
Shoeshine Johnson's legendary red bounty
bull, Killer Bee

The beautiful old chapel in Union Junction was filled
to standing room only. It seemed that everyone had
come to see Sheriff Cannady's sole child wed. Even
Delilah and the ladies of her Lonely Hearts Salon had
come to fill in as mother and sisters to Mimi. In fact,
they'd pretty much taken over the baking, the decorating and, Mason had heard, the choosing of Mimi's
trousseau.

According to Last—who'd been as thick into the
preparations as Delilah's crew, though that was more
the lure of the women than fascination with wedding
plans—the wedding-night nightie was a heart attack
of epic proportions.

Guaranteed to make a grown man go weak at the knees and rock-hard in the—

Mason forced his thoughts away from the dangerous wedding-night nightie. He shifted uncomfortably in the pew, thinking he'd rather be tied to a stake in the Alaskan wilderness with honey on his toes as a lure for wild animals. Anywhere but here in this flower-filled chapel. But, because of duty, for the sake of years of friendship, and for Mimi, he was here to see her marry another man.

His whole body felt strangely weak, weirdly ill and past the point of medical assistance. He was sweating through his black suit, and so nervous his feet were cold-prickling, as if straight pins were sticking through his shoes. Truth was, he was lucky as all get out that he wasn't standing up there in the groom's hot spot. Obviously, Mason was suffering vicarious wedding jitters, no doubt symbiotic, empathetic fear that was surely coursing through Brian O'Flannigan and telepathing to Mason.

How fortunate that I'm sitting here in the front row, the position of family favor, while he's standing there, about to be yoked.

He resisted the uncharacteristic urge to bite his nails. Crack his knuckles. Or even sigh.

His nine unmarried brothers sat beside him in the pew, their postures as rigid and unmoving as his.

Behind him sat Annabelle and Frisco Joe, as well as Laredo and Katy. The housekeeper, Helga, was baby-sitting Emmie at home.

Ranger had tried to talk to Mason about Mimi, as had Last. In fact, every one of his brothers seemed to think he was playing the coward's role, that he needed to do something about Mimi's marriage.

He had no intention of doing a thing. *She* was doing exactly what she should. Mimi and Mason were best friends, and no third party could ever change that.

Nor would Mason have changed it. One didn't marry one's best friend. No point in ruining a wonderful, since-childhood friendship by asking more of it than it ever could be.

Marriage was messy.

Not to mention he had nine younger unmarried brothers to look after. They might not be children, but sometimes they acted like it, and he needed to keep his focus on them. Add to that the fact that the family was now growing, with wives and children, and he had more responsibility than ever.

Matters were fine just the way they were.

And yet, when Mimi floated down the aisle on Sheriff Cannady's arm, passing by Mason with the sweetest, happiest smile on her face—she smiled *right* at him—her expression all glowing, it seemed heated pitchforks speared his heart. Pierced it to pieces.

God, she was lovely. More beautiful than he'd ever realized.

Maybe all his brothers were right. Maybe he did have his head lodged firmly in an unmentionable part of his anatomy. He meditated on this as the ceremony progressed, not hearing any of the words being spoken until the minister's voice rose dramatically, perhaps even pointedly.

"If any person can show just cause that Mimi Cannady should not wed Brian O'Flannigan, speak now or forever hold your peace."

The chapel was deathly silent, so eerily still that Mason could hear his own heartbeat *thud, thud, thud* in his ears. His suit went from merely hotter-than-hell to a prison of boiling fire as every eye in the church seemed to pin itself on him. Even Reverend Kendall glanced his way, though surely not with any meaning behind it.

Speak now or forever hold your peace.

He tapped his fingers on his knee.

Say it or forever keep a doofus, Uncle-Mason smile on his face every time he saw Mimi, which would be often, since she'd be living right next door, like always. He'd smile when she became pregnant. Smile when she proudly watched her children take their first steps. Smile when she taught them to ride their ponies. When she had birthday parties for them. When she grew gray and contented with her husband, forty years from today.

Speak now or forever hold your peace!

Mason cleared his throat.

Chapter One

Ranger Jefferson had never seen such a case of pig-headedness in all his life, but Mason won the prize, if there was such a thing. How could Mason have let Mimi get away the way he had?

Too much was happening too fast around the Union Junction Ranch. Even too much for Ranger. More-over, if he didn't get away from his twin's silly e-mail romance with a woman in Australia, he was going to go as cuckoo as a Swiss clock himself.

He couldn't stand it another moment. Without telling any of his brothers, Ranger had made a decision: It was time to join the military.

Okay, so he was no spring pup at thirty-two. But there were wars being fought all over the world, and the least he could do was volunteer for the National Guard. Maybe more.

He aimed to find out. Throwing his duffel over his shoulder, he headed out the door toward his truck.

"Where are you going?" Helga asked him.

"Shh," he told her. "It's a secret."

"Helga doesn't like secrets." She frowned at him, and he smiled back, eager to keep on her good side before she roused Mason. Mason believed Helga was the perfect housekeeper, hired by Mimi Cannady not too long ago, though nothing could be further from the truth. Helga was horrible, and Mimi had enjoyed knowing there was no cute young thing keeping house for Mason.

Of course, Mimi was married now, and that meant the Jefferson brothers could ditch Helga!

Helga's eyes narrowed on him. "I am making sauerkraut and sausage for dinner. Will you be back?"

Ugh. That decided him. His brothers would have to figure out a way to send the housekeeper packing on their own, if they weren't all still too stunned that Mason hadn't managed to belly up some bravery, to throw himself down on his hands and knees and marry the only woman who could ever love the pig-headed man. "I won't be back, Helga," he said. "Shh," he cautioned her again. "Mason needs his rest."

Well, that was the deciding factor. Helga adored Mason. If Mason needed his sleep, sleep was what he would get.

And Ranger would be long gone, his goodbye note of military aspirations beside Mason's breakfast dish. Mason wouldn't like it; he hated the fact that one by one, his brothers were leaving the family ranch, something he'd always feared.

But life had to move on, and no way was Ranger

going to end up like his twin, Archer, e-mailing some dopey girl in Australia. Or like Frisco Joe, whose leg had to be broken to get him to marry a wonderful woman. Frisco Joe and Annabelle were expecting a child, a sibling for Emmie. Of course, Annabelle looked real sweet pregnant, but…Ranger certainly didn't want to end up like Laredo, either, who had to get himself concussed by a bull to make him see the light about Katy Goodnight.

If body parts were going to get busted when it came to women, he darn sure wasn't going to let it happen to *him*.

The military would be a whole lot safer.

He hopped in his truck, quietly pulling down the drive and away from the only home he'd ever known. Just a couple hours away from Union Junction was Lonely Hearts Station, and the women of Lonely Hearts Salon. When his older brother, Laredo, had left Union Junction back in March, he'd made the mistake of stopping into the Lonely Hearts Salon to say hello to the women who'd helped the Jefferson brothers and most of Union Junction through a terrible February storm.

Laredo had gotten roped into a rodeo, and then marriage. The concussion had come in between.

Ranger was smarter than that. On his way to the nearest military base, he was going to drive straight through Lonely Hearts Station, Texas, without stopping.

No waving. No hello shouted through the window.

Last month, when he'd been helping Laredo learn how to ride the Lonely Hearts Salon's champion bull, Bloodthirsty Black, he'd met Hannah Hotchkiss, and she'd just about made him think twice about his narrowly divided world. He'd also met Cissy Kisserton, an employee of a rival beauty shop, who'd also made him think twice about life as he knew it. The two women had just about come to blows over him, and he'd liked it!

But…not enough to sacrifice a bone or a body part.

"There's bad luck in that town," he said to no one in particular as he sped down the highway, happy to be heading east and away from the ranch. "I'm too cagey to get caught in that heart trap. All that love business is a mess! Lonely Hearts ladies, Never Lonely Cut-n-Gurls—it's a soap-opera city. I'm passing through there at top speed!"

RANGER'S PLAN WORKED—until he saw the tall blonde waving at him in front of the Never Lonely Cut-n-Gurls Salon. "Dang it!" he muttered. "I *almost* made it."

Cissy Kisserton pulled open the truck door and tossed a silver-foil suitcase inside. "Thought I recognized your vehicle, Ranger. How fortunate for me, because I was about to hitch to the nearest highway."

Ranger couldn't imagine Cissy having trouble finding a ride. Yet he still didn't want to be the one to give it to her. She looked devastatingly gorgeous in skin-tight jeans and a cutoff T-shirt—dressed down for traveling and yet still packing dynamite.

"Shew!" he said under his breath. "I don't know where I'm going," he told Cissy.

"Neither do I. We'll get wherever together."

"But I may be stopping at the military base east of here!"

"Cool," she said. "I love a man in uniform."

He frowned at that. "I was planning on traveling alone, actually." No point in letting this silvery female use her wiles on him—there might be a busted limb in it! This town wasn't lucky for men.

"Lonely is bad, Ranger. We've learned our lesson about anyplace with the word *Lonely* in it. And we simply can't let you travel alone." Cissy tossed another suitcase into the truckbed, this one leopard-printed.

"We?"

"Hey, Ranger," Hannah Hotchkiss said, poking her tousled head around Cissy to smile at him, that devastatingly bright, cute-rocker-girl smile that had caught his attention the first time he'd been to Lonely Hearts Station. His heart hit his boots. These two women had nearly reinvented the catfight, bringing it to new form over him! Well, maybe not so much in the physical, girls-mudwrestling fantasy he'd had about the two of them, but that was something he would keep to himself. He didn't want both of them in the truck with him. There might be *two* busted parts of his anatomy in his future!

Cissy crawled in the front seat, ignoring his frown. Hannah jerked open the door to the extended cab. "Uh, Ranger, did you say you were traveling alone?" Hannah asked.

"Well, I *was.*"

"Well, you *weren't,*" she said, mimicking his tone. "There's a man in your back seat."

He whirled around, his jaw dropping when he saw his twin grinning up at him from his napping place in the back. "Archer! What in the *hell* are you doing?"

"Heretofore, I've been listening to you cuss all the way to Lonely Hearts Station," Archer said with a grin. "But now that we've got seatmates, I'd say this trip is going to be a whole lot sweeter!"

Which just showed how little his twin knew.

THEREIN LAY THE RUB, Mason told himself, which was a pretty stupid expression. What rub? he asked himself sourly. What fool had time to sit around and think up such stupid sayings?

The fact was, he was feeling testy, and he knew it, and his brothers knew it, though they hadn't complained as yet. Actually, they *had* complained—to each other when they thought he couldn't hear them. But they had spared him their grousing, and he knew why. Pity. Plain and simple pity, which was worse than if they'd just come right out and chewed his butt.

Mason sighed, pulled his hat down lower, and stared into his coffee cup. At this moment, he was only fit company for his horse, and so the barn was where he sat. And the word of the day was *moping*. He was moping—couldn't call it anything else—something he'd always told his brothers they weren't allowed to do. So he was hiding out here with Samson, because the horse wouldn't tattle on him and didn't care anyway as long as his hay was fresh.

"You like having me around, doncha?" he asked Samson softly, running a hand over the horse's back. "Not like *some* people I know."

Mimi. Mimi, Mimi, Mimi. Why did his mind always come back to her?

"And therein lies the rub," he said to Samson. "Not the kind of rub you like. The kind that really sticks in my craw, that makes my gut churn. I guess," he murmured on a deep sigh, "I guess I'll only say this to you once, and to no one else, but seeing Mimi walk down the aisle with Brian tore my heart right out of me. I thought I could handle it. I thought it wouldn't matter. But, ol' pal, it mattered. It just about mattered more than anything in my whole life."

It mattered so much he could barely show his face anywhere. The whole town knew, of course. Everybody had known that he loved Mimi. He just hadn't known it. He so much hadn't wanted to admit it to himself.

"And there are reasons for that, but none I'm going into, even with you," he said with a last gentle rub over Samson's back. He swiped his coffee cup and headed to the house. There were some things he wasn't going to think about—some fears not worth mentioning.

THROUGH THE MAIN HOUSE window, Last watched Mason as he left the barn and walked toward home. "Talk about a sore head," he muttered to Tex. "That one's a walking case of soreness."

Tex peered at Mason moving slowly toward the house, his gait not as firm as it once had been. "Why in the hell didn't he stop her?"

They both knew the "her" was better left unnamed. "Because he couldn't," Last said. "Mason couldn't stop Dad from leaving. He knew some people do what they have to do sometimes, regardless of what other people need or want. And Mimi couldn't wait around forever. Lord only knows, Mason was never going to marry her. And we all realized that."

"It would have taken a miracle," Tex agreed. "I am never falling in love. Never. It's much easier just to sleep with a woman who only wants sex." He leered happily until he caught another glimpse of Mason's face, set in sad lines. "And that's another thing I can't figure out. Why didn't he just *sleep* with Mimi?"

Last gasped. "Have you lost your mind?"

"Well, *hell*," Tex complained. "He *wanted* her. Even if he acted like he wanted an arm-shave more."

"Yeah, but she's like our little sister!"

"But that was the problem," Tex insisted. "I think he knew his feelings toward her were stronger than that, but he thought that was sacrilegious or some-thing.''

''But he couldn't have *slept* with Mimi,'' Last ar-gued, still horrified. ''That wouldn't have been right. I mean, Sheriff Cannady's daughter!''

''Well, then.'' Tex returned to the toaster where he discovered he'd burned the bread to a crisp. Smoke came out, and a disgusting odor. ''Hell-on-fire,'' he complained. ''Helga's gonna kill me. I've messed up her domain.''

Last shrugged, watching Mason kick mud off the porch that one of the brothers had scraped from their boots. ''If you ask me, life is going to get a lot mess-ier around here, more than any of us would like.''

And it was all Mason's fault. Unfortunately, as Last and Tex had just discussed, Last really didn't have an answer for what his big brother, Mason, *should* have done. All he knew was that whatever *needed* to be done hadn't *gotten* done, and now they were all forced to live with the consequences—except Ranger, who had escaped. *Traitor.*

''Where's Archer?'' Mason demanded as he walked into the kitchen.

''I ain't my brother's keeper,'' Tex replied, his voice instantly tense. ''Make that plural, just so you'll know.''

Last stared at Mason. ''What do you mean, where's Archer?''

''His roll-up tent and sleeping bag are missing from the barn storage.''

Last groaned to himself. One more brother on the lam. Whether Mason wanted to admit it to himself or not, he was driving his family away one by one—just as he had Mimi.

And Mason couldn't stop them from leaving—any more than he could have stopped their father, Maverick, from leaving when Mason was seventeen.

That's what love did to a man.

"It's not going to happen to me," Tex swore quietly, so that no one heard him except Last, who didn't need to be told what he meant. *"Never."*

Last nodded. Maybe it was better if love didn't hit any more of them. So far, in their family, love was a disastrous affair with biblically epic consequences.

"We're doomed," he murmured to himself, seeing the stone-carved expression on Mason's face.

"Doomed."

Chapter Two

Hannah Hotchkiss stared at the back of Ranger's head. She could practically see plumes of fire shooting right out of his Western hat. A man that temperamental ought to be a crime! He should be happy for the chance to sit next to Cissy—seemed like all men dreamed of being near her. But no—just like every other Jefferson male she'd met, Ranger had to be different and alarming and hypnotizingly macho. A sin in boots. She sighed to herself.

"I suppose you're pretty much bred from the Jefferson stock," she said to the man sitting next to her, a man who looked just like Ranger, which was startling and unnerving. The basic difference between them was that Ranger wore a brown Western hat, and this man wore a black felt with silver rope braid. The confident Jefferson smile was dashingly displayed, and the dark eyes were roaming her cut-open tennis shoes and funky-punky red-tipped hair with interest—she groaned silently with frustration.

And here she thought she'd been going to Mississippi to get away from memories of Ranger. Oh, no, life was not that simple. She had to discover he had an unnerving double.

The grin on her seatmate's face widened as he shoved his hat down over his eyes. "I'm going back to sleep," he said. "Ranger, you old dog."

In the front seat, Ranger stiffened at his twin's words. "I don't know what *that* means," he said, his tone annoyed.

Hannah rolled her eyes, but the twin kept his mouth shut. Cissy flipped her silvery hair and peered over the seat at the twin.

"Is he always such a wagon-load of joy?" she asked Ranger.

"It's a family trait," Hannah said, matching Ranger's sourness. "Tall, dark and intimidating."

"Hey!" Archer shoved the hat back and stared at her. "Don't lump me in with him. We're not twins in personality."

"Don't insult the driver," Ranger stated, "or you'll all find yourselves on the road with your thumbs out. Not much traffic at this hour, I might call to your attention."

Cissy patted his arm. "We're not insulting you, are we, Hannah?" she said with a warning glance. "Hannah's just playing around."

Hannah shrugged. The difference between her and Cissy was that Cissy came from the get-more-bees-with-honey school and Hannah came from the call-it-as-you-see-it school. The two schools operated so completely differently that it was a wonder she and Cissy had hooked up to get out of Lonely Hearts Station. But necessity made strange bedfellows—or truckmates, anyway—and both of them wanted out, neither of them had a vehicle and each agreed a female traveling alone was a recipe for disaster, never mind which school of thought one had graduated from. So they joined forces, decided to walk or hitch to the bus station—after leaving goodbye notes for Marvella and Delilah, their respective employers—and put themselves on the street with their luggage.

"Just playing around," Hannah agreed, looking at the back of Ranger's stubborn head, as Cissy gave her a thorough warning stare. "Don't take me too seriously, Ranger."

He snorted. Hannah pulled a baseball cap from her duffel and shoved it on her head, deciding to emulate Archer by closing her eyes. It was going to be a long ride to Mississippi, especially sitting next to the twin of a man she'd kissed and lost a piece of her heart to.

And it wasn't any easier knowing that Cissy had kissed Ranger, too.

"IT'S ALL YOUR FAULT," Marvella said to her sister, Delilah, as she held out Cissy's farewell note. "I hope you're happy with running off my prize girl."

"I didn't run off anyone," Delilah said with a shrug. "I lost a girl, too."

"Not like Cissy. Cissy brought in more customers than any other hairstylist I had."

"And it wasn't for her ability with hair," Delilah said. "Not that I'm partial to one of my girls more than another—they're all daughters to me—but Hannah's spunk is going to be missed around here. Far as I can see, Cissy wasn't any more special than Hannah, so quit acting like you lost something more valuable than I did. Anyway, I knew nothing about their plans, as you can see." She held out the goodbye note from Hannah, but Marvella ignored it.

"I should sue you for lost business."

Delilah sniffed. "Try it. Then you'll have to reveal exactly what your business includes, Marvella. Nobody's quite sure exactly what all's going on at your salon or why you need a monster-size heated spa."

"Massages and aromatherapy, just like the big city," Marvella told her. "Nothing fancy. Just pretty girls and relaxation at the end of a hard day for the menfolk. Don't make it sound so sinister."

Delilah had her doubts that it was so innocent, but that wasn't the point at the moment.

"One of my girls said she saw a truck stop to pick up Cissy and Hannah," Marvella revealed. "It was too dark to be certain, but Valentine said it looked like Ranger Jefferson's truck. Now, you can say that's a coincidence, that there's a lot of trucks around these parts, but we all had a good look at what the Jefferson boys drove last month. They all flaunt those extended-cab, super-size, my-wheels-are-bigger-than-yours stud machines. And I want you to know two things," Marvella said flatly. "One: I aim to find my best girl and bring her back. Two: If I find out it *was* a Jefferson boy behind the wheel of that truck, I'm holding you personally responsible since you brought those boys here in the first place. This town's not been the same since you went on your little sightseeing junket and came back towing those grateful cowboys. You've barely convinced me you weren't behind this little midnight rendezvous, but I'll still blame you if Ranger Jefferson snuck off with Cissy."

"Sister," Delilah said softly, "I haven't had much to do with you since you accused me of stealing your husband. Now you're claiming I had something to do with your best shop girl heading out. Frankly, I'm done talking to you. I can go another twenty or so years before we speak again."

Delilah closed the door, pulling down the blind. Sighing, she walked into the kitchen where Jerry, her truck driver friend-in-need sat, his face set in sympathetic lines.

"Did you hear that?" Delilah asked.

"Every word." He patted the chair next to him. "Sit down and let me warm your coffee."

She did, appreciating his willingness to care for her. "You're always here for me, Jerry. How lucky I am that you came to my shop instead of Marvella's."

"Naw. How lucky I am," he said, placing the warmed-up coffee cup in front of her. "Aromatherapy gets up my nose."

Delilah laughed. "You wouldn't have noticed it with all the girls in skimpy outfits just waiting to fix you up."

"Nope," he said, leaning over to kiss her on the cheek. "I got little enough under my cap that I don't need a cut often, and I can trim my own beard. But the best part of being here is the chocolate chip cookies, and the coffee." He gave her a twinkling eye as she lifted a brow at him. "Though the company's what really brings me back every week. Couldn't find that across the street."

She smiled at him. "Thank you. I needed to hear you say that." Glancing at the note in her hand, she said, "So. I'm down a girl. I guess that's a good thing, considering I had to cut my staff in half two months ago."

"Heard those gals you had to let go are rocking it in Union Junction. Stopped through there last week to check on them, and every last one of them is happy in the salon they started. And the Jefferson brothers are fixing up the house for them real nice."

Delilah nodded. "That just leaves me to figure out why Hannah suddenly up and left me. It's just so unlike her to be ditzy."

"Think it was the love bug." Jerry emptied his coffee cup.

"What love bug?"

"The one she caught for Ranger Jefferson when he was here helping Laredo ride Bloodthirsty Black last month."

''I didn't know she'd caught a bug,'' Delilah said, surprised. ''Seemed like she was totally focused on helping Katy metamorphasize into the woman-she-could-be to catch Laredo.''

Jerry shrugged. ''And at some point, Ranger got under Hannah's skin. Only Hannah thought Ranger liked Cissy, so she gave him a wide berth. Hannah's a firecracker when she's made up her mind something's one way or the other.''

''But now Cissy's gone and Hannah's gone, so that means they struck out together. I just don't imagine the two of them would willingly share a truck with Ranger Jefferson. Marvella can't be right about that.''

The phone rang in the kitchen, and Delilah answered it.

''Hey, Mason. Fine, everything's fine here.'' Her eyes widened as she listened, giving Jerry a stunned glance. ''No, Ranger's not here. Neither is Archer. Haven't seen either of them. Okay. Will do. See you this weekend.''

She hung up the phone. ''Malfunction Junction's missing two cowboys. Twins. Mason sounded like he was standing in a pot of boiling water.''

Jerry started laughing.

''It's not funny,'' Delilah said, her good mood totally shot. ''The four of them'll not last long in the same truck. It's a volatile mixture, and I wish Hannah was back here where she belongs before she gets her feelings hurt!''

"DOES DELILAH KNOW you've gone?"

Hannah's eyes met Ranger's in the rearview mirror of the truck. Dark and expressive eyes. She should have been able to read his thoughts.

It annoyed her that she couldn't. She'd never carried on a conversation with Ranger from *behind*, and she couldn't measure him without being able to see the rest of his face or at least his posture—it was hard enough to feel comfortable around him when she could meet him face forward. Prickling ran down her arms and tingled her neck.

"Hannah," he said. "Does Delilah—"

"Heard you," she replied quickly, realizing his tone was telling her a lot, mainly that he thought she was ignoring him. "I left Delilah a note."

The dark gaze left the road and met hers in the mirror again for the briefest of moments. "Did something happen to make you leave?"

I fell in love with you and had to get away from here knowing you didn't feel the same about me. And did you have to kiss Cissy?

Dumb question. There wasn't a man alive who could resist Cissy.

That didn't mean she had to be Heartbroken Hannah. "Did *you* leave *Mason* a note?" she snapped back.

His eyes hooded.

"Then I assume nothing in particular happened to make you leave." She settled herself in her seat and stared out the window. Beside her, Archer cleared his throat.

"I didn't leave a note. I signed my name to the pithy message Ranger left beside Mason's plate," he offered.

She turned to stare at him, as did Cissy. Archer shrugged. "Seemed like Ranger said everything that needed to be said."

"I said I was going to join the military," Ranger stated. "Did you actually read it before you John Hancocked it? Not writing your own note seems rather lazy, by the way, for a man who nearly wore his fingers out hitting the send button to Australia."

"Easy, bro," Archer said mildly. "Ye ol' love life is none of thy concern."

Hannah shook her head, perplexed. "Besides Mason who works hard, and Frisco Joe who figured it out, and now Laredo, who's moved to North Carolina to be with Katy like a real man would, are all of you pretty much rascals?"

"And relationship-dysfunctional?" Cissy put in. "It's almost scary that the two of you could be in the same truck and not know it."

"How was I to know that my twin was a stowaway?"

Cissy shrugged. "I heard twins had some special extrasensory perception for each other. Y'all seem to be blocking your ESP."

"Heaven forbid he could have just asked for a ride," Ranger complained.

"Heaven forbid you could have offered," Archer rejoined.

"Did I know you'd be up for the military?"

"Did you think to ask?" Archer demanded. "Why did you think you could leave me behind with His Highness the Hardheaded?"

Cissy and Hannah both turned to face Archer again.

"Well, that's what Mimi calls him," Archer said sheepishly. "Mason, that is, before she quit hanging around our place."

"She probably had to leave out of self-defense," Hannah said. "Your family isn't exactly easy for a woman to bear."

In the mirror's reflection, she saw Ranger's eyebrows peak over his eyes. "How would you know?"

Caught, because she didn't want to admit that her feelings had been hurt by Ranger, Hannah said, "Keep your eyes on the road, cowboy. All of us want to reach our varied destinations safe and sound."

"And I want to talk about your destination," Ranger stated. "Where exactly are you two going?"

Cissy turned completely to face Hannah. "I don't know that it's such a good idea to tell him. They're just going to say that we don't know what we're doing."

"You said it for me," Ranger pointed out. "I think it, I know it's true and now you've put it out in the open. We're all prepared for my reaction, so just say it: What's your end-of-the-line destination?"

"I called a friend of mine who runs a gambling riverboat in Mississippi," Hannah said. "Cissy and I are going to be hostesses on the boat. Well, I'm going to be a card dealer. I got Cissy a job as a hostess."

Both men started laughing, immensely amused by the revelation. "Going to the good ship, *Lollipop*," Archer sang, until Hannah's annoyed expression brought his tune to an end.

Ranger turned the truck at an exit ramp, parking at a truck weigh station and rest area. "Okay," he said sternly. "All ladies out of my truck. I ain't taking you any farther than this."

Cissy hesitated, but Hannah popped right out of the truck. "Fine," she said. "I can get a better-looking, more polite and chivalrous ride, anyway. One that doesn't poke his nose in my business and then laugh."

"Archer laughed, I just—"

"Same thing. All you Jeffersons are alike. It's your way or the highway. Well, I," she said with a deliberate glare at Ranger as she tugged her leopard-print duffel from the truck, "don't even think you're that hot of a kisser."

"Huh?" Ranger and Archer said at the same time.

"Now wait a minute—" Ranger began.

"Kisser?" Archer stared at his twin. "Did you kiss her?"

"Technically, it was a peck," Ranger began.

"He pecked both of us, then," Cissy inserted. "Only my kiss went beyond the peck category, I feel certain."

"You kissed her, too? And they're both riding in the same vehicle with you?" Archer grinned over the seat at his twin. "No wonder the atmosphere in here has been decidedly icy. Brr."

Hannah didn't want to hear about the kissing Cissy had gotten from Ranger, but knowing that the man was such a fast-and-loose kisser was the main reason she didn't want to let her heartstrings get pulled any tighter. Obviously, her kiss hadn't meant anything to him.

"I knew this was a bad idea. Cissy, I vote we call Jerry. Sooner or later, he'll be by this way in his rig. We should have done that in the first place, I guess."

Maybe, but she and Cissy had agreed between themselves that burdening anyone with their departure wasn't fair. And, frankly, they were afraid they couldn't say goodbye if they had to face down a couple of salons full of friends. And Cissy would have had to say goodbye to Marvella—no easy thing, considering Marvella would have thrown a fit.

But for Hannah, saying goodbye to Delilah would have been impossible. She couldn't have said goodbye, and she wouldn't have. In the end, she would have stayed—always captive to the hope that Ranger would return. Call. Ask her out. Remember their kiss.

Ranger crossed his arms at her, and Hannah felt her heart sink a little deeper in her chest. Did he have to be so handsome, even when he was being so dreadfully bossy? "Go," she told him. "Head off. Don't waste my time giving me the omnipotent eye."

"The omnipotent eye," Archer mused. "Isn't that what Helga does to us when we put our boots on the coffee table?"

"Can I speak to you alone for a moment?" Ranger said to Hannah.

"I don't see why—" she started, but Cissy gave her a shove and Ranger gave her arm a pull and she was heading off toward a picnic table with Ranger before she'd finished her sentence.

"Look," he said, sitting her down on the plank seat. "Have you thought this through?"

She thought she heard concern in his voice, real concern, and it startled her out of her indignation. "Yes, I have. And you can stop looming over me like you know everything and what I know could fit into a thimble."

He stared at her. "I'm not looming."

Okay. So at over six feet he couldn't exactly help his proportions. She'd wanted to be able to read his posture, and now she certainly could. "So. How long did you think about your road trip?"

"A while."

"I don't remember you mentioning it before."

"We didn't talk much."

No, they hadn't. Mostly, she'd wanted to kiss him. And that peck comment had hurt her feelings, because it had been more than that to her. "Where are you going?"

"I'm going into the military." He gave her a most belligerent glare, daring her to laugh.

Which she did. "Okay, that's it," she said. "Get back behind the wheel and stop harassing me about my spur-of-the-moment plans."

"Hang on." He put his boot on the bench beside

her and leaned forward. "I'm a man, and you're a woman."

She cocked a brow at him. "Continue. So far, you're astounding me with your powers of observation."

"What I'm saying is, it's one thing for me to be heading off into the wild blue yonder. Joining the military is an honorable, responsible way to work through this phase of my life. You, on the other hand, are going off willy-nilly, shady-lady, to get a job as a card dealer in a floating casino. That is not a particularly admirable thing, not that I'm making any judgment calls here." He held up a hand to ward off her rebuttal. "I just don't know that it's safe. And maybe you know that it's not such a good idea, or you wouldn't have snuck off like a thief in the night without telling Delilah."

"You're big-brothering me, and I don't like it," Hannah told him.

"Not exactly that," he admitted. "Since I kissed you, I feel a bit more responsibility than the average Joe, I guess."

"You called it a peck," she reminded him, her indignation clear. "A peck. If you pecked me, what did you do to Cissy?"

"Now, Cissy," Ranger immediately rejoined, leaning back to grin at her, "that girl can suck the lips off a man's face. She takes a man's breath and makes him feel that dying in her arms is a good thing."

"Really!" Hannah hopped to her feet. "You know what? I've had enough of your bellyaching and your grousing. You get us to the state line, and that'll be just fine, Ranger Jefferson. And you can just let the military have your sorry self. Maybe they can kick some sense into you.''

She headed toward the truck without waiting for him to reply. Ranger stared at her retreating red-tipped blond hair and saucy backside as she flounced off. He raised a brow. ''Baby, baby,'' he murmured. ''I do believe that little gal is jealous.'' And then he grinned.

RANGER QUIT GRINNING by the time Archer and Hannah decided they had something in common. Snug as two bugs in the back seat, they taught each other their best tricks at cheating in card games.

It was bad enough, Ranger thought sourly, that his twin was full of bad ideas and tomfoolery. Of course, it was all in the spirit of fun, under the guise of *tricks,* but he didn't think it was a good idea for her to know any more tricks than she already did. Her repertoire was astonishing. Where did such a little spitfire learn so many sideways maneuvers?

Worse, he didn't want Archer teaching her anything, card tricks notwithstanding. And he sure as hell didn't like the repetitious, nerve-grinding, unnecessary bursts of laughter from the back seat.

Those two were becoming way too close for his comfort. And they were having way too much fun, playing reindeer games in the back seat while he sat up here like a chauffeur. Ranger's teeth ground together. That's what it sounded like: reindeer games. Childish. Immature. His twin was leading Hannah astray, and she was going there with a smile on her face.

"Don't you think the two of you have played enough games?" he demanded. Cissy glanced up at him from the magazine she was reading, and he gave her a sidelong glance that was empty of the irritation he felt.

Hannah and Archer ignored him.

"Gotcha!" Hannah squealed, moving fast to grab something from Archer's side of the truck. He moved to elude her and cards went flying over the seat and everywhere else. It was snowing diamonds and hearts, and Ranger's temper snapped. "I can't drive if you two are going to keep acting like monkeys in the back seat."

Archer looked at him. "Cool it, bro. We're not bothering you."

Oh, they were bothering him a lot. His gaze met Hannah's in the mirror. Ever so pointedly, knowing he could do nothing about it, to show her utter disdain for his comment about monkeys, Hannah stuck her tongue out at him.

No one else noticed, but that wasn't the point. The woman was set on bothering him. She was going to make him pay for his remark about Cissy. He shouldn't have said it, especially since he'd colored what happened between him and Cissy, but it was too late to take back his exploratory quest into Hannah's jealousy. Now she was in top wild-filly form.

And that naughty pink tongue drove him nuts.

"I'd offer to drive," Archer said, his tone not serious at all, "but it's more fun to sit back here with Hannah. Deal, lady."

She gave Ranger one last pointed glare in the mirror before the sound of shuffling cards shredded his nerves.

Great. The two of them were having the time of their lives. And he sat up front with Cissy Kisserton, who really hadn't sucked the lips off his face at all.

Hannah Hotchkiss was just about the most annoying woman he'd ever met!

A burst of laughter erupted from his twin, and Ranger decided enough was enough. "I think I'll take a break here. Give everybody a chance to stretch." He pulled the truck alongside a historical marker, well off the highway. The road's shoulder was thin, and below, a beautiful canyon stretched as far as he could see, dry and majestic and peaceful. Ranger felt his brain start to compress to a normal size. He took a deep breath, determining that he could forgive his twin anything. He smiled at Cissy, who had so far borne her seatmate's bad temper without complaining.

He could even feel more jovial toward Hannah. "Let's get a beer out of the back of the truck, and we can all sit back there and munch. We can even play some of those card games you love," he told Hannah as kindly as he could, in an effort to be forgiving toward her for everything she'd done to him. He could be a good host. He could be fair and eventempered. "Card games and icy beer sounds like a great combo, doesn't it?" he asked the group at large as he clambered into the truckbed. "And could you ask for a better view?"

Hannah followed his lead, clearly not certain to what they owed his new, improved mood. He set the cooler in the middle of the truckbed, pulled out beers for everyone, closed the lid and pointed to the faux table top. "Deal," he told her. "Any game you like."

"I'm best at strip poker," she told him.

He choked on his beer. It went down hard on his Adam's apple, making him mad all over again. "Strip poker! Hannah Hotchkiss, are you trying to drive me insane? Because if you are, you're…you're…" He stopped when he saw the incredulous stares on Cissy's and Archer's faces. Belatedly, it came to him that she'd been teasing him, getting his goat. Janking his chain—which was a cross between a jerk and a hard yank.

He had to admit she'd janked him pretty good.

Well, he could jank a pretty mean chain himself. "Strip poker? Go right ahead. Deal me in, lady."

I'll just love seeing you lose.

Chapter Three

"I don't think so," Hannah said narrowly. "I really don't trust this sudden change in you. I'll sit in the truck. Thanks for the beer, though." She hopped into the back seat.

Archer shrugged and joined her. "Guess I'm not in the mood, either. Maybe after a few more hours on the road."

Cissy grabbed her beer and slid into the front seat. Ranger glared after the three of them. "Now, look," he said. "All of you are riding in my truck, on my gas money. Archer, you're a stowaway, and you ladies are hitchhikers. That means I get to call some of the shots." The good mood he'd tried to work himself into was totally, completely gone.

Archer pushed his hat back. "Okay, boss. What do you want us to do, besides play cards? We're happy to earn our keep somehow. I'll chip in the gas money for me and the gals. How's that?"

Ranger liked that even less. "The gas money isn't the point."

"What is, then?" Hannah asked, staring up at him with those ridiculously innocent eyes, and that perky hair just flying away all over her head like it had training in getting his attention.

Like Hannah and her antics with Archer. None of them understood him. Now he knew why Crockett was always moaning that no one appreciated his artistic bent or the beauty in the nudes he painted. He empathized with Bandera, who spouted Whitman like a dervish and claimed his memory-driven talent and Shakespearian oration were underrated by his brothers. He could even see why Tex got so frustrated when his brothers laughed at his buddus interruptus problem—buds that wouldn't bloom—in their mother's rose garden.

It hurt to be misunderstood. And he just didn't want to say out loud what he really felt.

But he was going to have to do it. Somehow.

"I think it would be best if you and Cissy changed places," he primly told Archer.

"Why?" everyone asked at once.

Irritation spiked his brows. "Because it would just be best for the sake of *propriety.*"

Archer's expression said Ranger had lost his case with that one. "You're beginning to sound like an idiot, bro."

Hannah blew a huge bubble with pink gum, let it pop and blow back against her lips. How could any woman drink beer and chew bubble gum? It was weird. It was amazing. Disquieting. And it made him think about her pink tongue and her pink lips and her red-tipped dirty-blond hair. And sex.

Sex with…Hannah.

"Have you always had mental problems?" she demanded. "I've never heard so much nonsense in my life. How can riding in the back seat have a lack of propriety about it?"

"I can't see you clearly," he complained.

"We're not doing anything exciting," Hannah told him. "Nothing any more exciting than you and Cissy are doing. *Currently*."

Maybe the edge in her voice was only heard by him, but it told him everything he needed to know. She'd been jealous of him and Cissy kissing, and now she was feeding him his own medicine with a large spoon.

Well, two could play at that game. "Never mind," he said cheerfully. "Miss Cissy, let me help you into the seat. Comfortable? Did I tell you how much I like you in those jeans? No girl wears jeans like you do."

And then he gave Hannah a big grin as he closed Cissy's door.

KNOCK YOURSELF OUT, Hannah thought to herself. Play your one-man band in Cissy's orchestra of admirers. I don't care.

She couldn't waste any time focusing on some ill-tempered male. Besides, Archer was proving to be very adept with card tricks. "Teach me that thing you did with moving the jacks around and pulling out a queen," she said to him. "It's a really smooth move."

"Only if you'll teach me how you know which card I pulled from the deck. I can't figure out how you're doing it," Archer said admiringly. "It's like you've got an extra eye or something."

Hannah smiled, and shuffled the deck.

THREE HOURS DOWN the road, Ranger had to admit his plan had totally backfired. He might as well be a professional limo driver for all the attention Hannah paid him. She and Archer laughed like hyenas, and they still hadn't worn the ink off those stupid cards yet. Well, they'd bent a few, so Hannah had merely reached into her duffel and pulled out a brand-new deck. This had set Ranger's neck muscles to Too Tight, just like an over-wound machine.

And then, to make the whole thing more annoying, Archer pulled out dice. The two of them had been clacking and rolling them, and blowing on each other's hands for luck.

It was all so disgustingly happy Ranger could only be grateful for the impending darkness. Then they'd have to quit their gaming, he thought with a mental rub of his palms.

But no. Archer pulled out a flashlight, aimed it at the roof of the truck as he jammed it into the seat to steady it, and they went on giggling like children keeping secrets from their elders.

Cissy closed her magazine and looked at him with

a smile. "We sure do appreciate you taking us this far. I thought for sure we were out of a ride back there at the weigh station."

He didn't want to be reminded of his bad behavior. "Naw," he said reluctantly. "I just hope you two have thought your new employment out fully. Mason would get all over me if I let either of you get hurt."

"We're not your responsibility, Ranger."

"Not technically, I know. But we feel that all of you gals who helped us through the big storm are pretty much our sisters now."

"I wasn't there," she reminded him.

"No, but Hannah was. And we know you. So we care about you."

She didn't say anything to that.

"In a brotherly sort of way, of course," he hastened to explain. "We care about you like a little sister."

It seemed to him that Cissy looked hopeful for a second. Then her impossibly large aquamarine eyes dimmed as she shook her head and re-opened her magazine.

"You sure have a lot of magazines in your bag," he pointed out.

"I'm taking up cooking." She smiled at his raised brow. "What? Didn't you think a girl like me would want to cook?"

He frowned. "What do you mean, a girl like you?"

She shrugged.

"Oh, you mean, a gorgeous girl like you!" he said,

his tone saying, I just got it. "The kind who's so nice guys are always fighting to take her out!"

The most grateful smile he'd ever seen on a woman's face lit Cissy's eyes. "You're okay, Ranger," she said softly. "If I can help you in any way with your mission, let me know."

"My mission?"

She barely moved her silvery brows to indicate the back seat, where neither Archer nor his partner in gaming was paying them any mind. "My little gamine friend," she said softly.

Oh, no. They were not going there. He might have discovered that Cissy had a lot of smarts underneath that sexy platinum hair, but she wasn't going to start reading his mind. He wasn't that easy. "She's not my mission. I'm joining the military to do my duty by my country."

She smiled.

"If they'll take me," he amended. "I am a bit older than they like."

"Hey, tough guy," Cissy said, closing her magazine to look at him. "Maybe I should swap seats with her."

"I like you right beside me. Don't even think about it. She'll just give me a heart attack, I'm sure. Death by arguing or something. Worse, she might insist on driving my truck, and then I'll have to show my really ornery bachelor side."

"As if she hasn't seen that already. And survived it. Who would have known?"

"Exactly," he said with a nod. "Hey, not exactly!"

Cissy laughed.

"How did you two get together anyway? I don't remember the two salons having many cross-street friendships."

"I didn't want to live Marvella's way anymore. I went to Delilah's to ask for a job. I met Hannah in the hallway. She'd been crying."

"Hannah crying?" Ranger scowled, the thought extremely unsettling. "I find that hard to imagine."

"It wasn't pretty," Cissy told him. "That cute little face all scrunched up and running mascara. She is not a pretty crier, I warn you. Of course," Cissy said with a sigh, "she'd been crying over some dopey guy, and that's probably what made her so pathetic. I mean, what man is worth crying over?"

"She was crying over a man?" Ranger asked incredulously. "Are you sure?"

"Oh, positively. She spilled the whole story about him. Boy, he really broke her heart."

"What a butthead," Ranger said hotly. "She deserves better than someone who's careless with her feelings!"

Cissy pulled a file out of her bag and began filing her nails. "I know. That's precisely what I told her. That's when she said she was going to Mississippi, and I said I could use a change of scenery, and presto-chango, here we are. Kind of funny how life works, isn't it?"

"Yeah. All except the crying part." It really bothered him that some boob had made Hannah cry. He
resolved right then and there to be nicer to her. She
was such a fragile little thing, always acting tough-
enough, like a pullet in a chickenyard, but he knew
better now, thanks to Cissy. Hannah was tenderhearted underneath that spicy attitude and paprika-
tipped hair. Why, he just wanted to hug her to him
and keep her safe and protect her from all the louses
on the planet—

Giggles ripped from the back seat, and Hannah
squealed as Archer grabbed her, wrestling her like a
dogie to the seat. Cards flew, dice rolled, and something that looked like a sandal flew through the air.
That was all Ranger's ping-ponging, bug-eyed vision
could see in the rearview mirror.

But whatever was going on back there, his twin
and that sweet tenderhearted pullet were having one
yahoo of a good time.

"Archer!" Hannah screamed, her voice delighted
with laughter. "Stop!"

It was a full-blown ticklefest in the back seat, and
from the sound of it, Hannah was on the happily losing end.

In the front seat, Cissy glanced at him without ceas-
ing her filing. "Let me know if I can help you. When
you decide to make your move, that is."

"There's going to be no move," Ranger said from
between gritted teeth. "At least, not from me."

Cissy nodded. "Fear of failure?"

"No." He glared at her. "Fear of the Curse of the Broken Body Parts."

"Which is?"

"My brother Frisco fell for Annabelle Turnberry. He got a broken leg. Laredo got concussed when he fell for Katy Goodnight. I've kissed both of you. That actually puts fear into me. There could be two broken body parts waiting for me. No, it's not fear of failure that sends me down the road, Cissy. It's healthy self-respect and self-preservation."

"You look fine to me so far. One piece, nothing missing. Nothing except a little spine, maybe. Just maybe. A small piece that could be mildly fractured and waiting for repair."

"Not a durn thing wrong with my spine, thanks."

"It's pretty obvious you feel something for her, Ranger," Cissy said softly.

"I feel protective. I feel brotherly. But nothing romantic, I assure you."

"Okay. But let me make certain I understand this. You'll know when love hits you by the amount of pain you suffer? Emotional masochism visited on the body in physical form?"

"To put it in my terms, doctor, if something breaks, I'll know it's the real thing."

The giggling in the back seat subsided for the moment. Ranger decided they'd used up their oxygen share back there.

"Of course it could be your heart that gets broken," Cissy said absently. "Which would be metaphoric, not a physical manifestation. And what would that tell you?''

''Nothing,'' he said as his eyes searched the rear-view mirror. He couldn't see a thing because of the darkness, but that didn't stop him from trying to see. It had gotten too quiet in the back seat.

''Where are we, anyway?'' Cissy asked.

''A few hours east of Lonely Hearts Station, but probably a couple more hours from the state line. Desert.'' Ranger peered into the darkness. ''The wind has picked up so much it's blowing sand against the windshield.'' Turning on the windshield wipers, he tried to clear the dirty glass.

''Where are we going to sleep?'' Hannah suddenly asked, leaning over the seat to eye him.

''Sleep?'' Well, that was something he hadn't thought about. When he'd left this morning, he'd figured on sleeping in his truck. He hadn't planned on riders. Women. ''I don't think there's a hotel anywhere around here. We're pretty far into the desert, I think. There haven't been any signs for miles.''

The thought of the four of them sleeping in the truck was unappealing, particularly as Archer would no doubt enjoy sleeping with Hannah more than Ranger would enjoy sleeping behind the steering wheel. Once again, Ranger felt an annoying spurt of jealousy heat the top of his head. ''I'll stop here and let you stretch your legs. Archer, if I can borrow my flashlight, I'll check the map and see where we are.''

Pulling down a deserted lane, Ranger switched off the truck.

"I'm too tired to stretch my legs," Hannah said. "I could go to sleep this second."

"Here. Lay your head *acquí*." Archer put a pillow in his lap and pointed for Hannah to lie down.

Ranger didn't think she would—and then, she did just that. It was as if she never gave a second's thought to what was lying *beneath* Archer's innocent pillow. Ranger's eyes practically popped from his skull. Glancing at Cissy, he caught her shrug.

"You still seem to be in one piece," she whispered as Archer sang Hannah a lullaby. "Guess you were right. She means nothing to you."

"Damn right." He ripped the map from the glove compartment and stared at it with the flashlight's dimming beam. "The two of you wore this flashlight out with all your hijinks," he groused, but no one answered. "Dang, that's a lot of wind," he said, glancing up to peer at the window. "I think we're in a sandstorm."

"That sucks," Archer said, his voice sleepy. "I'm hungry."

"You can reach through the back window and grab something out of the cooler," Ranger said. "I can't tell where we are, but it's nowhere close to civilization, I'm afraid."

"If you wait a little while, maybe the wind will quit blowing," Cissy said. "I'll take a snack, if you don't mind, Archer."

To Ranger's relief, Hannah popped right up and off Archer's lap. "I'll get you something, Cissy." Poking her arm through the window, she pulled back quickly. "Wow! That feels like a thousand needles hitting my arm!"

"Let me do it. I've got sleeves." Archer leaned up and snagged a bag from out of the cooler, shoving the lid back on quickly. "Pretty smooth, huh?" he said to Hannah.

"Yeah. Like you made good grades in Grabbing Stuff from the Truckbed 101." She peeked into the bag before glancing up at Ranger. "Twizzlers?"

"That's my kind of snack," he said. "Twizzlers and beef jerky. Nothing better."

"And tequila to wash it down," Archer said, happily examining the contents of a brown bag he pulled from underneath Cissy's seat. "Safe as a baby in a bank vault."

"Whatever," Ranger said sourly. "Grab the plastic cups from underneath my seat and pour, Archer."

The scent of tequila filled the truck. Archer handed Ranger a plastic cup full of sweet clear liquid. "Driver first, since we're parked for a while. Good limo-ing, dude."

Ranger raised his cup. "Here's to new beginnings. For all of us."

Archer swiftly poured for the rest of them. They raised their cups and clacked them against each others. The men swallowed their tequila in a gulp, while Cissy and Hannah sipped at theirs more gingerly.

''Now,'' Ranger said with a satisfied sigh. ''I'm a new man. And I'm ready to beat you at strip poker, Miss Hotchkiss.''

Surprise made Hannah hesitate for only a split second, then she pulled out her cards with a sly smile. ''I fancy your shirt, Mr. Jefferson.''

''I fancy yours, as well.'' And he fancied her jeans and her bra and her panties off her little body—but that was a fantasy for later. One day when they were alone, and he'd tamed her, and she liked it, and being naked for him was her only desire in life, then he'd win her panties right off her heart-shaped bottom and drink her like this tequila. He poured himself more tequila for bravery.

He was going to make Archer wear a blindfold. And then when Ranger won her shirt, he was going to be the happiest man on earth. The fantasy would start tonight, and it would drift like a fairy tale, page by page, day by day, article of clothing by article of clothing. Oh, yeah.

The tequila was warming him, making him unwrinkle. He stared at his cards, then at Hannah, who was watching him with a crook in her tricky blond brows. She didn't look as though her hand of cards was all that swift. Ah! Sweet victory was his! ''Pour me another, Archer,'' he said with growing confidence. ''Tonight is going to be my night!''

Chapter Four

Ranger awakened slowly. He felt odd. His eyes didn't want to open and his skin seemed strangely cold.

Very cold. Taking a deep breath, he forced himself awake and took stock of his body.

He was wearing nothing but a pair of black boxers.

He was in a jigsaw shape, stretched out in the two front seats, his body wrapped around the armrests and the console. It was the most uncomfortable position he'd ever been in. His body complained, telling him enough was enough.

Uncreaking himself to a sitting position, he looked into the back seat. Archer was in the middle, Hannah and Cissy curled up on either side of him, heads on his shoulders. Archer had an arm around each woman, and they looked warm and toasty as mice in a barn in winter. Completely snug.

They were all fully dressed.

Ranger's mood, sour yesterday, fermented to acidic. He didn't remember getting blammo'ed, but clearly he'd been that and lost at strip poker. Even nearly nude, he hadn't had a woman crawling up next to him. Which wasn't how his life usually went, and the problem was obviously Archer. It wasn't enough that his twin had to stow away on Ranger's mission of finding himself. Archer had to hog the women, too. The women Ranger had kissed.

And they'd deserted him for the comfort of the back seat.

Hannah could at least have pretended that Archer wasn't the best pillow since goosedown. She'd said she fancied Ranger's shirt. Well, she was sitting on it, a winner's taunt. His jeans were under Archer's boots, and his socks were just plain gone. "Why bother to stop at my shorts?" he groused. "Pity? Don't like black?"

Turning, Ranger faced the windshield. Sand still flogged the truck, telling him he was in for a good whisking if he stepped outside. But nature was calling, and he probably had enough tequila inside him to blunt the pain. There was no point in getting dressed, he decided. The sand would just lodge in his clothes. Better to get dressed once he was safe inside the truck again. He could dust off his body after he made the world's quickest pit stop.

Carefully opening the door just far enough for him to slide out, he hopped onto the ground, his bare feet landing onto something possessed of a million sharp needles.

"Yow-ee! Ai-eeee!" Jumping to get away from whatever the hell he'd stepped on, he tumbled downward, hitting rocks and weeds and unidentified things as gravity cruelly grabbed control of his world to dump him at the bottom of an abyss.

He was flat-assed. "I'm dying. I'm dead!" he gasped dramatically to the sky. "Deader than dinosaurs. Damn it, I've landed in hell!"

It was dark, it was cold, and it was very, very painful. His mouth and nose were full of sand; his skin was being burned by flying grains of fire. He had to find cover. And there was no way he could get back up to his truck—he'd rolled ass-over-ass forever. Pulling himself to a sitting position, shielding his eyes, Ranger realized he was in front of a stone enclosure. Dragging himself to the stone wall, he dismissed thoughts of bears and snakes. That type of danger was secondary to his bodily anguish. The enclosure turned into a cave, and he gladly fell inside, gasping from pain and fear and overwhelming loss of control.

Ranger knew, as he felt consciousness seep away from him and his breath cut short in his body, somehow, he was dying because of Hannah Hotchkiss.

"I'M DOWN FOUR MEN," Mason complained to Mimi as he perched uncomfortably in her kitchen. Sheriff Cannady was upstairs napping, Mimi had said, and Brian was running errands. "Frisco Joe, Laredo, Archer and Ranger."

"I'm sure Brian would be willing to help, when he returns," Mimi said.

''Can't do that to a man who's still honeymooning.'' The second he said it, he felt his face flush. *Honeymoon* and *Mimi* were two words he really didn't want connected in his consciousness.

He'd known Brian was gone—he'd seen the sports car leave. Brian was a nice man—under other circumstances Mason might have hired the lawyer himself— but the miserly courage he'd worked up was close to failing him.

It was all he could do to make himself bring over this belated wedding gift. Facing Mimi was pain and pleasure. He was so glad to see her—and he was so ripped inside. She was more beautiful than ever. ''Marriage agrees with you,'' he said gruffly.

She glanced at him, startled, hesitating as she pulled the tissue from the silver-and-white bag that encased his gift.

A long silence stretched between them as her eyes searched his. Why had he said that? His brothers said she'd always wanted to marry him. Not Brian. Not any man but him. But he hadn't even been able to comprehend marriage, much less to Mimi. And yet, not to anyone else but Mimi. His comrade-in-clowning. His best friend. His sister.

Marriage? Had she really wanted to marry him? Was she in love with him? He had to know.

And yet, the time to ask had passed. He saw that as her gaze dropped from his. She pulled the silvery tissue from the bag and smiled at his gift. It was a framed picture of her and all twelve Jefferson brothers, taken last summer when everything had still been normal. The men were dressed in jeans, hats and no shirts. Mimi wore jeans, a hat and a blue-and-white-checked blouse tied at her waist. There were six brothers on each side of her, but she was standing next to Mason, his arm around her waist as they all grinned proudly.

"I love it," she said softly. "Thank you so much."

"There's a gift certificate in there to the place where you registered your bridal stuff. I didn't know what you wanted most."

His fingers worked the brim of his hat; he couldn't meet her gaze. He was in hell.

He'd bought the ticket there himself.

"Speaking of honeymoons, I have a huge favor to ask of you." Mimi sat across from him at the table, her expression worried.

"Shoot." He could deny her nothing. Now, anyway.

"I know you're down on hands, but…Brian and I didn't take a real honeymoon. We got married and decided to plan the other details later."

He hadn't realized they hadn't honeymooned. He'd been too buried in a frozen mask of pain to pay attention. "I knew you got married fast."

"Yes. Very fast." She took a deep breath. "I really want this to work out, Mason."

His heart burned, but of course, she had no idea of his newfound realization of love for her. She knew she'd been his best friend. She would expect to be able to share what was on her mind now.

He'd buck up and offer the shoulder she seemed to need. "I know you want it to work, Mimi. You'd not have married Brian if you hadn't expected it to be forever."

She nodded. "I think the best thing we can do for our marriage is to spend time alone together. Brian hasn't asked me for it, because—" Glancing up at the ceiling, almost as if she could see through to the second floor, she said, "Well, he's just been so patient with me. But it's not fair to him."

Mason was lost, but he nodded to show he was listening.

"I've decided we need that honeymoon. So I've planned a trip to Hawaii for us." A shy smile lit her lips. "I've even bought a couple of bikinis."

Fire shot through his entire body. Hell colored his heart. "You'll be the prettiest honeymooning gal in Hawaii, Mimi," he forced himself to say.

She reached to put her hand over his. "It's a lot to ask of you right now, Mason, but could you keep an eye on Dad?"

He started to chuckle and say that it ought to be the other way around. Sheriff Cannady should be keeping the eye on him—but the seriousness in her blue eyes shut his mouth instantly.

"We'll only be gone a week, and if you could check in on him from time to time—"

"It's done, Mimi. It's no trouble, and it's done."

"We leave tomorrow night. Brian will be home tonight, and I'm going to surprise him with it. I mean, he knows we're going on a trip, but—"

Mason shook his head, realizing he was about to hear more personal details than necessary. Clearly, Mimi was feeling very anxious about her new marriage and eager to please her new husband. "You don't have to tell me a thing. Whatever you need is yours." He put his hat on his head, leaning down to kiss her cheek. The scent of roses touched his nose, and he thought about the days when the two of them were childhood friends.

Now they were adults. "You have a wonderful time," he told Mimi. "You and that new husband of yours deserve every happiness."

She smiled gratefully, but not with the elation a new bride should be wrapped in. Maybe the honeymoon would ease her mind. He would pray for that.

Mason left the kitchen, letting the screen door close quietly behind him.

INDIAN TOTEMS FLOATED around him, colorful and yet faded. Primitive drawings illustrated the beauty of emotion and life inside his mind. No, the totems and drawings were outside his mind. Ranger came to in a sweaty fog, realizing someone sat beside him, cross-legged. "Hey, I know you," he said to the apparition. "I saw you in *The Last of the Mohicans.* You're the Native American that got stabbed and tossed over the cliff. Your wife was none too happy about that, by the way.''

The dark-skinned man raised a brow. ''You have a fever,'' he said quietly. ''You've been hallucinating.''

''You're real.''

''Yes, but these are the first coherent words you've spoken. At least, reasonably coherent.''

Ranger frowned. ''Then you weren't in the movie.''

The man shook his head. ''No.''

''My name's Ranger Jefferson.''

''I know. And I know all your brothers' names, and their every fault. I also know that you are in love, and this scares you terribly.''

''Nope.'' Ranger closed his eyes. ''Now you're hallucinating. I am not, nor ever will I be, in love. It's dangerous in our family. We're cursed. It all started when our mother died. Or maybe it started before then. I haven't been able to figure that one out.''

''Hmm. Drink this.'' The man offered a tin cup to Ranger.

''If that's a love potion, I'm not thirsty,'' Ranger said stubbornly. ''You have to understand, I'm already in bad shape. I need to keep my wits about me.''

''By all means,'' the man said dryly. He put the cup beside him. ''My name is Hawk.''

Ranger checked the man's bare feet, colorful poncho and leggings. "I would have thought it was something fancier, but never mind. Can you get me out of here, Hawk? My buddies are around here somewhere."

"They're in your truck, sound asleep."

"Still? It's been hours! They should be looking for me by now." A sudden thought occurred to Ranger. "Hey! How did you see my truck? It's too far away for you to see from here."

Hawk laughed. "There's an easier way to get up and down the arroyo than the route you took, friend. Anyway, they're fine. I'm sure they'll come looking for you soon. What happened to your clothes?"

Belatedly, Ranger realized he was covered with a rough but warm blanket. That and his black boxers were all that kept him warm—and clothed. "It's not worth talking about," he said, embarrassed.

"First, I figured she kicked you out. Otherwise you wouldn't have babbled about her so much in your sleep. Then I realized it was your pride that had sent you down here. You should rest," Hawk said, waving a hand over Ranger's eyes. "You should reflect upon the bad feelings inside you."

"Now look," Ranger said impatiently, aware that sleepiness was claiming him and not sure what Hawk had just done to him with that hand trick but knowing Hannah would be all over it like a curious kitten, "I have no bad feelings inside me. I stepped on something sharp and lost my balance."

"A poison plant," Hawk clarified. "I picked the needles from your feet. The poison can kill you."

"And so could yapping with strangers." He fought the darkness.

"You have more to fear from yourself than me." Hawk gazed back at him patiently. "Have you heard that saying about having to hit rock bottom before you can start back up? Metaphysically, you have hit rock bottom by rolling down into the arroyo. Best you don't return to your truck and your woman until you examine your life."

"My life's fine." Ranger closed his eyes.

"You're running."

The voice sounded far away. Ranger relaxed, actually glad that Hawk was keeping him company.

"Your father left. You're leaving. But people sometimes leave to get well. You have left to stay unwell. One day, you must choose to heal yourself."

"Listen, when I want a shrink, I'll call one. Now let me sleep. And tell my brother to get his ass down here and get me."

But something was wrong. He couldn't move his arms or legs. He couldn't think straight. And it was true what Hawk said, most of it anyway.

Not the part about being in love, of course.

HANNAH GASPED when she saw the shape Ranger was in. "He's like, red!" she exclaimed.

Hawk nodded at her. "Yes. An after-effect of the antidote I gave him. He would have died."

"Oh, thank you," she said, wringing his hand gratefully.

"He's still got a long way to go," Hawk warned her and Cissy and Archer, who looked suitably concerned about his twin.

"Should we get him to a hospital?" Archer asked.

"If you like. Unfortunately, they are not familiar with how to treat these types of illnesses. And the nearest hospital is two hours away." Hawk looked at the waning sun outside the cave. "My advice would be to let nature take its course."

Hannah dropped to her knees beside Ranger. "We stopped here because of the sandstorm. It was impossible to see anything. Which is how he stepped on the plant."

"It would have helped to have had boots on," Hawk pointed out, not a trace of sarcasm on his face. "Clothes. Of course, he suffered lacerations rolling down so far. I fear infection."

"He lost at strip poker," Hannah admitted. "Even Cissy can beat him, and she's not that good at cards. He gets huffy when things don't go his way."

Hawk smiled. "He needs time to let the fever pass by."

"You know what you're doing?" Archer asked.

"I have treated this before."

"You some kind of doctor or something?"

Hawk gave a bland nod.

"My grandfather was a medicine man. I inherited some of his skills and many of his medications."

"I know who you are," Hannah said suddenly. "Red Hawk was your grandfather. He was a famous medicine man in this part of Texas. I remember reading about him in the newspaper."

Hawk nodded. "It's true."

Hannah stared down at the thrashing cowboy under the blanket. For the first time, she began to feel panic, and a little forgiveness seeped into her soul. Not too much forgiveness, because he was still a louse for kissing Cissy, but she didn't want him to be sick. "Can you help him?"

"Do you want me to?" It seemed his eyes asked her for another answer. "Do you care?"

"I want him well. He's ornery and pigheaded, but I don't wish him ill."

Hawk glanced at Cissy, but then knelt at the side of Ranger. He placed a palm over Ranger's face. "The fever is very high. But I will do my best."

Ranger's eyes snapped open, staring and glazed. "Maverick isn't coming back, bro," he told Hawk.

"I know." Hawk nodded as if they were indeed brothers, and as if he knew who Maverick was.

"I'd better go find him."

"Someday." Hawk pushed Ranger down gently. "Sleep now."

But Ranger's gaze had found Hannah. "I'm dying," he told her. "Just like the dinosaurs."

She gasped. "Don't say that!"

His head rolled to the side. "Marry me."

"What?" Hannah stared at him, her shock greater than her worry right now.

"You have to marry me so I won't die."

"Wait." The forgiveness zapped right out of her heart. "Look, cowboy. You said the Curse of the Broken Body Parts would visit you if you fell in love. So far, nothing's busted on you, so let's stay ahead of the game. I am not about to believe that I am your cure for a hot head and pierced feet."

"I have to marry you," Ranger insisted. "Cissy read one of those girly magazine advice columns to me, and it said that marriage can actually make someone healthier. It has to do with dopamine."

"You *are* a dope." Hannah shook her head at Hawk. "He's lost it. Could the damage be irreversible?"

Hawk didn't answer.

"*You* marry him, Cissy," Hannah said, standing. "Although I've never heard of a wedding ring curing anything."

"I have," Archer said. "People do it all the time. A joining of souls makes each half of the union stronger. It's like…it's like spirit healing. Internal buffering against inner demons. Double-taping a pipe for strength, if you need an illustration."

"Hannah," Ranger said on a gasp. "Say yes. I know what I'm doing. Those lovelorn columns all say a man just needs the right woman to change his world. His whole outlook. And a married man is the happiest and healthiest species of male on the planet. They live the longest. Say yes!''

"Oh, all right," Hannah said crossly, not meaning it. Pacification was the plan at the moment. He wouldn't remember this absurd conversation later, anyway. "Yes."

"We didn't all hear you," Ranger stated, his tone determined. "Witnesses."

"Yes!" Hannah exclaimed, totally annoyed. "But just to save your life." A sigh of exasperation left her lungs. Trust that when she finally got a proposal from the man she loved, it was because he saw her as a tool to his own well-being. "Now go to sleep, Ranger. You need to break that fever, or I'm dragging you into a city for conventional medicine."

But no one paid her last words any mind. Hawk put a rope wedding band on Ranger's left ring finger and took Hannah's hand to tie an identical ring on her finger. He murmured some guttural words, moved his hands over both of them and then closed his eyes.

"What's he doing?" Hannah demanded of Cissy.

For once in her life, Cissy seemed at a loss around a handsome man. "I don't know. Hawk, are you all right?"

"Maybe a good shot of penicillin might be best for Ranger—" Archer said, stepping forward.

Hawk took Hannah's hand and placed it inside Ranger's.

Instantly, the angry redness left Ranger's skin. He closed his eyes and went to sleep.

"Hey, he turned into a human rock. What just happened?" Hannah demanded.

"The fever left him," Hawk said with a broad smile. "Apparently, you are good medicine for this cowboy."

"Lovely," Hannah said. "Just lovely."

"That was amazing," Archer said.

"That was a miracle," Cissy said.

"It's what happens when two people surrender their spirits to each other," Hawk said, satisfied.

Hannah stared at the rough rope ring on her finger. "Okay, that was a Hallmark movie moment. For his sake, I hope the cure takes, I really do. However, I really can't use a husband while I'm dealing cards on a riverboat," she told Hawk. "When he's well, can you undo this thing?"

Hawk nodded, looking worried. "It's not a good idea. Unjoining is unhealthy."

Hannah could think of more unhealthy things. "So is hanging around until the sand hits the fan. What happens when he snaps out of it and realizes he's tied to the one thing he wanted the least?"

"Ranger *is* pretty much of a rascal," Cissy said, worried. "He's going to think she somehow tricked him into this. Ranger is the only man I know who says he doesn't want to be married and means it."

Archer blinked. "They have a point. Can we leave him here with you for a while? We could head on down the road, and maybe you don't mention what cured him. When he's a hundred percent, you could ship him back to Malfunction Junction.''

Hawk shook his head. "He needs her close by."

"Well, three hundred miles is close enough," Hannah pointed out. "Our spirits can dial in long-distance."

Hawk grinned. "Now I know why his aura changed colors when he saw you. You are the right woman for him. He runs, you run. Together, you can run like wolf mates."

Hannah shook her head. "Even if I believed that there was a right person for everyone on the planet, I can assure you that the man under that blanket wearing nothing but black boxers is not my destiny."

"He's your husband," Cissy reminded her. "Sort of."

"Yeah, well." Hannah went to stand at the mouth of the cave, looking out to where the sand had finally settled, leaving the arroyo dusty. "Not for long."

Chapter Five

"It's come to my attention," Archer said to Cissy as he slid next to her on a rock under the stars that evening, "that there's no huzzah-huzzah between you and me."

She couldn't help looking surprised. "Should there be?"

He grinned. "Not that I know of. I just thought I'd mention it."

"So it's mentioned. What else is on your mind?"

"The fact that my twin is married for the moment. You and I are not."

"Right-o," Cissy said with a nod. "And it's staying that way."

"Precisely. I vote we ditch them."

Archer now had her full attention. "Ditch...your brother? And my traveling buddy?"

"Hey. It only sounds cold. There is a method to my madness."

"Not an obvious one."

"Look, we've already established that we're safe alone together."

"Much safer than even you can comprehend after your stupid suggestion. Like I would ditch Hannah," she scoffed.

"Hmm. Honor amongst rival hairdressers. I didn't factor that in," Archer said.

"Maybe you should have factored in honor amongst brothers. Then you might have had a measurement by which to gauge your witless idea. Let me weigh this out." She held up two palms, pretending to hold something in each. "Turncoat in this palm. Brother in this. Turncoat. Brother. Hmm, I think blood outweighs personal agendas every time, Archer."

"So do I," he said eagerly. "You've misunderstood my goal."

"You want to leave a sick man and a woman without a cell phone in a canyon cave with a stranger. What was the goal I didn't get?"

"They need to be alone together—in order to give their marriage a chance."

"Archer," Cissy said, enunciating her words, "they are not really married. It's a ruse, while Ranger is out of his head. Their union is as flimsy as those rope rings."

"Shh! Don't let Hawk hear you say that!"

"Why not?" She shrugged as he glanced around nervously. "He was very clear about that mumbo-jumbo being a psychological edge more than anything.''

"Yes, but there's a possibility the marriage could take, if it's given a running start."

She crooked a brow. "You'd want that?"

"Uh, yeah. You don't know what it's like to live in a house with no women. Hannah will fit right into our family. She'd like us. We'd take real good care of her."

Cissy frowned. "I don't think Hannah has that in her cards, so to speak. She was more excited about getting out to the riverboat than I was."

"Well, she just needs some time with my twin. He'll change her mind."

"Okay. Let me see if I follow. You and I are going to hit the highway and take off somewhere."

"You and I can head in the direction of the riverboat scene. If Ranger and Hannah decide they don't like each other, they can catch up."

"Why does this seem unfair? You were the stowaway. He was the man with the mission. And you're planning to leave him behind."

"Marriage could be his mission, if we give him a chance to find out. Don't you think? We could be adding to the successful outcome."

"His or yours?"

"Both. Look, I was in the back seat having a snooze. I didn't know my twin was planning a road escape. I was just looking to get away from Mason for a while. There's almost no place to get away from him these days, so I picked the truck. Next thing I know, the truck is moving and I'm about twenty miles down the road. Ranger's talking to himself, muttering like a madman. Should I have left my bro to his own devices? Not me. I figured he needed someone to help him through his trauma. If you lived at Malfunction Junction right now, you'd understand the necessity of brotherhood.''

''Mason is that bad?'' she asked with a frown. ''He seemed nice enough when he came to the rodeo.''

''It's not only Mason. It's Helga the Horrible.'' He sighed deeply. ''She keeps us on our toes to the point we can't ever relax. And she is devoted to Mason. He returns the feeling. The rest of us don't get a vote, but if we did, she'd be voted out.''

''I heard there are two other houses on your property. There's also a new hair salon if you were of a mind to have some female companionship for a while. Sorry, Archer. I'm just not buying all this pitiful me, let's take off and leave my brother behind. What's your real reason for wanting to leave him behind?''

He eyed her hopefully. ''Being alone with you?''

''Sorry.'' She shook her head. ''I'm in love with another man.''

That thought seemed to give him pause. ''Do I…know him? It's not Ranger, is it? That would explain your unwillingness to desert him.''

''It's not Ranger.''

''But…I know him. You didn't say I didn't.''

She turned away, guarding her gaze. ''Archer, I

don't know you very well, and…we don't really need to be having a conversation this personal.''

"The thing is, I think Ranger really likes Hannah. He needs to be alone with her if anything is going to be achieved.''

Cissy faced him again. "How do you know that?''

"Because he wanted to marry her.''

"To get well. Bottom line, he's using Hannah because he's hallucinating. I'm not leaving my friend for that reason.''

"Uh-uh. He asked for her. Any girl might have worked the spell, even you. But no sparks flew between you two. But now, him and Hannah, they just about set the whole truck ablaze.'' He looked at her for a moment, then took a deep breath. "Look. I'm leaving. I'm taking the truck. I didn't want to leave you behind, because you don't fit in the picture. You'll just be a third wheel. You're safe with me, because there's no…um, attraction between us. But if you want to stay by Hannah's side, so be it.''

"But wait. What are they going to do for food?''

"Hawk has supplies. And I left Hannah some of those magazines of yours. The ones with the recipes in them.''

He started walking up the hill. Cissy bit her lip, then glanced toward the cave. Was he right? Did he have a point? Or was he simply being a rolling stone?

Yet, he didn't strike her as being totally irresponsible. A bit chauvinistic, maybe. But guilty of one-upping Ranger, no.

''Wait,'' she called, running after him. ''Where are we going again?''

''To that riverboat of yours. Hannah can catch up with us there. When she gets Ranger over his fever. If she still wants to find Mississippi.''

They struggled up the rock incline together. He never turned to offer her a hand, and she appreciated that he let her take care of herself. ''Shouldn't we say goodbye?'' she said on a gasp of exertion.

''Defeats the point,'' Archer explained. ''Hannah would freak about being left alone with him. Remember, she was a very reluctant bride. I do believe she'd abandon him in a heartbeat. Don't you think she's probably the kind of girl who finds it difficult to be honest with herself?''

''I think if you see that in her, it's because you recognize it from self-examination.'' She grabbed hold of a boulder and heaved herself up onto the road. ''I think you should know, she's planning on discarding him the instant he's upright.''

''I know. I was amazed that she agreed to do the rope-ring thing at all.''

Archer followed, his breath heavy, as well.

Beside the truck, waiting with a grin and a duffel, was Hawk. ''I told you there was an easier way to get back to the truck.''

''I must have missed that part,'' Archer said.

''Well, possibly I told your twin. No matter,'' he said cheerfully. ''You owe me a ride.''

Cissy blinked. ''How do you figure?''

"All that down in the cave," he said with a wave of his hand. "A real doctor would charge you. I'm only asking for a ride."

"Don't you have a vehicle?" Archer asked curiously.

"Yeah, but I'm going far away. There's no place to keep it. I'll be back one day, but I don't know when."

"Hold on a minute." Cissy held up a hand. "You're going to leave a sick man here alone?"

"He has his wife," Hawk pointed out, "the conveniences of my cabin and my truck keys. What more does a man need in life?"

"Your cabin and your truck keys?" Archer repeated. "Did I miss something?"

"Cabin's up there," Hawk said, pointing his finger up a large hill toward a forest of dense, skinny trees. "So's the truck. You didn't think I lived in that cave, did you?"

"Yes," Archer and Cissy said at once.

"Nah." Hawk threw his stuff into the truckbed. "I do anthropological studies on the Native American totems and relics. It's family history, but it's also Texas history. And it's important. But I'm ready for a long break. And I left them a note about using the cabin. Promise. They were sleeping like babies when I left, all fever gone. So," he said with a glance at Archer, "can I horn in or is this a private party?"

"No," Archer and Cissy said together.

"Hey. We're getting good at that," Archer said. "We think alike."

"Only when we're saying no. Archer and I are not having a private party, and I don't care if you horn in." Cissy climbed in the front seat. "But I'm driving, fellas. My mother always told me not to get into a strange car with stranger men."

She pulled her blond hair into a knot and waited with her hand out for Archer to give her the keys, which he did.

"I'll flip you for the front seat," he told Hawk.

"I'd rather sit in the back, actually."

"So would I," Archer said, "she's a bit temperamental for such a beautiful woman."

"She does have a healthy spirit. I might not be man enough to handle it."

Archer snorted. "Same. She did say she was in love with someone—" He looked at Hawk suspiciously. "It couldn't be you, though. We just met you."

"True," Hawk said cheerfully. "That's okay. I'm just looking for a ride, not a woman. I'll sit in the back. You look like the type that gets carsick if he sits in the back seat too long."

"I—" Archer blinked, realizing he'd been roped into something he didn't want to do. And in his own brother's truck!

"Come on, Archer!" Cissy called. "We're not making a very clean escape!"

That was true. Archer jumped into the front seat

next to Cissy. "Bye-bye," he said to his twin. "See ya on the wild side!"

"You're really enjoying this, aren't you?" Cissy started the truck and pulled off.

"I am." Archer closed his eyes. "It's not every man who gets to do a good deed for his brother. Trust me, Ranger wasn't going to realize he was in love with Hannah until he was stuck with her."

"He wanted to marry her!"

"That was his subconscious speaking. You don't think a rope ring and some vows uttered by a fledgling medicine man-amateur anthropologist are going to hold Ranger to a state of wedded bliss, do you? All bets are off when his brain kicks back into gear. Trust me. All of us Jeffersons have very strong control over our subconscious desires!"

RANGER SAT UP, realizing he felt like a new man. "Hey, look. No red. No fever."

Hannah turned to give him a narrow eye. "Hey, look. No Cissy. No Archer. No Hawk and no truck. We've been dumped."

He brushed sand from his hair and then from his shoulders. "They've probably gone to run an errand."

"I don't think so. There's Hawk's knife."

A hunting knife held down a note, which lay on top of her leopard-printed duffel and Ranger's duffel. "Feel free to use my cabin and my truck. I'll be gone for a few months on a tracking mission for a missing person. Sheets are clean. Best of luck. Hawk,'' Ranger read. ''That's generous of him.''

''Considering we don't want to use his cabin and his truck, I don't find it that generous. And Cissy was supposed to be my friend. My new sister-in-hearts.'' That was the unkindest cut of all. She'd been deserted by the one person she'd thought she could trust in this adventure.

''They probably figured I wouldn't get well for a while. And you're my wife, so you're supposed to nurse me. Right? That's what they would think? I mean, if you look at it that way, them leaving doesn't seem all that wrong.''

''Hey.'' Hannah turned, her red-tipped hair askew, her lips swollen and chapped from the wind. ''I'm not your wife. You're well, so it's over. Okay?''

He stood, and she held up a hand. ''Keep that blanket securely around your waist.''

''You've seen me in my boxers before.''

''Yes, but we weren't alone before. And we were drinking tequila. It seemed all right then. It doesn't now.'' She turned so he couldn't see the blush on her face.

''I like modesty in a woman.'' He reached for his duffel and pulled out some jeans.

''I don't care what you like,'' Hannah said tightly. ''It's great that you're better, so now we can move on with our lives and quit pretending.''

''You saved my life. I'm your servant forever,'' he

said playfully. "See? I'm even going to put on a shirt."

She burst into tears. "Stop playing around!"

"What?" He was genuinely confused. "Hey, come here." Gently, he pulled her into his arms.

"No." She shoved herself away from him. "You don't understand. You nearly died. And you were talking like an idiot. All that marriage stuff was weird. You were weird. I didn't like it."

"Oh, you're stressed." Ranger nodded wisely. "You didn't want to lose me."

"No, I really didn't care about that," she said with a sniffle.

"Oh." She'd totally stuck a fork in his ego. "You weren't worried about losing me? Then why are you crying?"

"Because I thought you might die. And you talked me into doing something bizarre. You said you never wanted to get married," she said accusingly.

"I didn't. I don't." He shrugged as he put on his shirt. "So what's the biggie?"

He really didn't get it. "The biggie is that we did. And I didn't want to. But you scared me, and so I had to. You and that freaky Curse of the Broken Body Parts thing. You didn't even break anything! It was all just inflamed!"

"True." Ranger looped his belt into his jeans and shook out his boots. "And now I no longer believe I'm susceptible to the curse. Clearly, it has bypassed me."

''So?'' She was afraid to hear the answer.

''So we can get a pretend divorce to undo our pretend marriage.''

Of course that's what he would say. He tricked her into marrying him using false pretenses. It was sort of like, you show me yours first, then I'll keep mine a secret. She'd been cajoled into showing her feelings first—and then when he'd seen her hand, he trumped her.

That's what happened when a person loved someone who didn't love them back. You lost.

Not that she'd ever believed that he loved her, not for a second. He'd only been interested in saving his skin. And she'd kept her guard up, knowing it would never work out. Still, her guard had not been enough to protect her heart. ''Good,'' she said, raising her chin, ''here's your ring back.'' She pulled the rope ring from her finger and tossed it at him, but it landed on the ground between them.

''Feel better now?''

His brows raised as his dark gaze inspected her face. She felt as if he could see her real feelings, the hope he'd dashed to pieces inside her. ''I feel excellent. Thank you for the consideration of the inquiry.''

''Hmm.'' Turning from her, he lifted both the duffels and walked to the front of the cave. ''Coming?''

''Might as well,'' she bit out. ''This sure isn't a honeymoon.''

''Hey, we're divorced, remember? Now we're just backpacking buddies. Off to the cabin we go. I'm curious to see what kind of accommodations that charlatan of a medicine man has.''

''He saved your life,'' she reminded him. ''You could be a little grateful since no one thought you'd be ignorant enough to step on a poison plant and nearly kill yourself rolling down an embankment.''

''Quite an adventure you've had with me,'' Ranger said cheerfully, leading as she followed. ''And you thought you had to get to Mississippi for excitement.''

She rolled her eyes.

He laughed, which grated on her nerves. It was if he'd never been ill.

''Actually, I credit you with saving my life,'' he called over his shoulder. ''You could have left me, but you didn't. You could have not married me, but you did. I've had buddies that were less loyal than you, Hannah.''

''Great. I feel like a Saint Bernard.''

He laughed again. ''Just about another mile, and we'll be up there, among the clouds.''

''I want a long bath,'' she warned him.

''I'll scrub your back.''

''I don't *think* so,'' she bit out under her breath.

He'd kissed her, then he'd kissed Cissy. He'd married her to heal himself, and then divorced her as soon as he gained his feet.

No way was he going to lay one finger on her body. ''I've got Hawk's knife, and I know how to defend myself,'' she reminded him. "I saved your life, and you're my servant. You can fix dinner while I soak.''

"Sounds like someone has a fantasy they'd like to share.''

"My fantasy is that we part ways sooner rather than later,'' she said, irritated. "That's the only way you'll ever figure into one of my fantasies, Ranger Jefferson.''

SHE WAS MIFFED, and Ranger knew Hannah had every right to be. He'd waylaid her from her trip, she'd had to nurse him and now she was stuck with him. At least until they could figure out what kind of wheels Hawk had. Ranger was doing the big, silent man act, but inside, he couldn't believe everything had gone as badly as it had. It seemed that from the moment he'd picked her up, he had lost his way with this woman.

Now the crazy little strawberry-tipped blonde was off him good.

And that bothered him. Nagged at him. Was beginning to eat at him.

Why? He couldn't figure that. She didn't like him. If she did, she hid it better than any woman he'd ever known. Women flirted around him. They brought him food. They left things so he'd have to return them. Sometimes they sent him letters with lipstick kisses, sprayed with perfume and, once, containing a thong.

Hannah ignored him. In fact, she'd just sprouted tears over the fact that she'd married him, even though it had proved to be good medicine. Hannah wasn't playing around. It was in the stiff set of her shoulders; the determined look-away of her eyes. She was hopping mad with him.

And he badly wanted to get into her good graces.

His ego slid into his boots.

He had no idea how to go about it.

"THE PROBLEM IS," Hannah said as they walked into the cabin, "that this is wasted on us."

It was simply the most adorable cabin she'd ever seen. Who would have guessed Hawk lived so romantically? If she'd been able to design a heaven among the clouds, it would be this cabin. The decor was navy and white, softly, thoughtfully entwined, like clouds. A soft, plumpy sofa curved around a fireplace. Candles sat everywhere; there had to have been a hundred gold ones set in groupings throughout the great room. Walls of windows encased the entire room, giving the effect that here one lived above the trees and just below the stars. "It's so romantic," she breathed.

"Imagine what it will look like at night." Ranger tossed their duffels onto the white-carpeted floor. "We can do some major stargazing just sitting on the sofa."

Hannah shivered, thinking about stars and night-time and Ranger. "There's a telescope near the balcony."

"Mmm." He looked in the fireplace. "And gas logs. Ecologically minded guy is our Hawk."

"Did you think he'd be the tree-burning type?" She scratched her arm. "I'm going to find the kitchen. I'm starved. If he's got pretzels, I'll be thankful. That's all I ask for. Pretzels and some cold water."

The kitchen was an elaborate chef's paradise, with copper pots hanging from a rack in the ceiling and a small stairway leading into a wine cellar.

"Oh, boy." Ranger reached in and snagged a bottle. "Shall we have wine with dinner? Or at least wine?"

There was a note on the fridge. "Hannah and Ranger," she read, "allow me to fix the first meal that you share as honeymooners. It's not much, but I had to think quickly. You'll find a chicken spaghetti casserole in the fridge. Heat at 350 degrees until bubbly. Enjoy the wine cellar. Hawk."

Hannah could feel a blush sneak over her cheeks. "He thought of everything."

"Yeah, I feel like I'm at a resort. Won't he be disappointed when he learns we won't be sharing a meal as honeymooners?" Hawk popped the wine cork and poured two glasses.

"He'll be gone for a few months. He won't ever know. And I can eat fine under false pretenses, thank you. Pop that in the oven, since you said you were cooking. Although it seems to me you've gotten off the hook. I'm going to go bathe." She snatched up her wineglass and left the room.

The master bedroom was beautiful, with mahogany wood and soft draperies decorating a room that looked out over the trees. However, it was the master bath that left her breathless. "Hey, Ranger!"

"Change your mind so soon about wanting me?" he said as he walked into the bathroom. "Whoa. That is a bathtub made for two. Maybe four."

"I've never seen anything like that in my life." Hannah picked up a bottle of bubble bath that rested on the edge of the marble. "Crabtree and Evelyn. You know what?" She glanced up at Ranger.

"You tell me. I'm not knowing much of anything right now."

"Something's fishy with this Hawk guy. If he had all this up here, why did he leave you in the cave when you were ill?"

"Because he couldn't have dragged me up here without a crane," Ranger said sensibly. "And he didn't know us. I mean, we could have been ax murderers, for all he knew."

"True," she murmured. "But doesn't all this seem extravagant? For one man? A recluse?"

"I don't know. I don't care. I'm jumping in that tub if you don't. Hey," he said, as if he'd just had the thought to end all thoughts, "why don't we get in there together to conserve water? Have you heard that filling a bathtub takes more water than the average shower?"

Hannah held up her hands. "I'm soaking alone, sans you."

He eyed the tub. "But we'd fit in there so nicely. You're going to be lonely."

"Trust me. I'll be enthusiastically lonely."

His eyebrows raised.

She sighed. "You are so starting to scare me. When did your brain kick into sex drive?"

"I don't know. Maybe since we got married? It must have been the fever. I wasn't like this before."

"Oh, yeah. You were. I distinctly remember you slinking into the Never Lonely Cut-n-Gurls salon. And since you don't appear to have had a haircut in oh, maybe two years, I think it's safe to say you went there for another reason."

His dark gaze trained on her. "You don't trust me."

She shrugged. "Go away. I'm going to make a friend, otherwise known as a washcloth puppet, and scrub my feet. After that sandstorm experience, I'm starting to rethink wearing tennis shoes with cut-out toes. You think they have sandstorms around here often?"

"Hannah, I kissed Cissy once. It was no big deal."

"Is everything 'no big deal' to you, Ranger? Because that's what you say about everything." She looked at him, unwilling to acknowledge the pain inside her. If he didn't care, she sure wasn't going to.

He seemed surprised by that. "Do I?"

"Yes, you do. And it comes so easily to your lips that I believe you. Nothing is a big deal to you. Not kissing Cissy, not kissing me. Not leaving your brother in the lurch, not marrying me because you had a psychotic brain twitch. It's all 'no biggie.'"

She turned the faucets on and poured in bubble bath. When she turned around, Ranger was gone.

"Served him right," she murmured to herself. "Big baby."

WHEN HANNAH came out from an hour-long soak, she felt like a new woman. And the aroma floating in from the kitchen had her stomach growling.

But it was the great room that took her breath away. Every single candle in the room was lit. It was as if a hundred stars burned against the velvet of the night sky outside the windows. The table was set, and two wineglasses waited beside china plates.

Ranger took her in at a glance, his eyes nearly as bright as the candleglow. "Hannah," he said, "I'd like to change your mind about 'no biggie.'"

Her knees trembled a little at the intense look in his eyes. She felt like prey stumbled upon by a wolf.

"And then there's that matter of my psychotic brain twitch," he said, drawing closer. "Now, psychosis is something I've never been diagnosed with before, and I was wondering," he said, taking hold of her hand, "if the nurse who nursed me in the cave is in? Because I haven't thanked her yet for taking such good care of me."

He took her face between his palms, and Hannah's tremble kicked up to tremor. The pieces of her broken heart rattled against each other with expectation, with hope. Gently, he brushed his lips against hers, never taking his eyes from her astonished gaze.

"You look scared," he murmured. "We've kissed before, remember?"

"Peck," she said. "You called it a peck."

"Well, this time," he said, lowering his face toward hers again, "this time, it's a kiss. And it's going to be a 'biggie.'"

Chapter Six

"Wait," she said, moving her head back just before Ranger could kiss her, hating that she had to do it and yet knowing she had no choice. She couldn't allow this romantic hideaway to lure her into a spell. "This is a bad idea."

"No, it's not. Hold still." He winked at her, then drew her forward again.

"No. I'm serious, Ranger." She pulled away, making certain his hands fell from her face and completely broke their contact. "One of us has to be."

"I'm serious. I seriously want to kiss you."

"I know. Me. And Cissy. And whoever comes along next."

"Not that I'm arguing the point, but you didn't exactly seem reluctant before."

She gazed at him before going to sit on the plump sofa, in a spot where his charm couldn't work on her. "Hey, I recognize boredom. Remember me? I'm going to work on a riverboat to give me a change of scenery."

"I'm not bored."

"You're the king of bored. You left the ranch because you were bored. You decided to join the military on a whim, knowing you were probably too old to be accepted. But actually, you just wanted an excuse to leave."

"You're going deep on me again. This is in the same category with the brain twitch or whatever it was."

"Not really. Boredom is the same reason you kissed Cissy, and it didn't mean anything. And then me, and that didn't mean anything, either. You're having a midlife crisis."

"Midlife crisis?"

"That's what I think."

"From your powers of observation as a hairdresser."

He was irritated, but she'd expected that. She was, too.

"And my observation as a card dealer. I learned to read people. It's not too hard to read that you're bored. And I don't have a sign on me that says, 'Looking for fun? Hang out here for a while.'"

He sighed. "Okay. You're right. It was a bad idea. I shouldn't have tried to force a romantic issue."

She watched him carefully. "You agree with me? Really?"

"This time, yes."

"I mean, I don't even know you," she pointed out.

"Well, you knew me well enough to kiss me before."

"You said peck. We pecked."

"Pecking is between friends."

"Can be. Yes." She nodded emphatically. "Very sisterly, even."

"Gotcha." He sat on the sofa at the opposite end and crossed his legs up on the table. "So, you ready for me to warm up Hawk's truck?"

She blinked. He'd probably spent ten minutes lighting all these candles. "You want to leave? Do you feel up to it?"

"Sure. If you do."

The dinner smelled good, and the cabin was warm and pretty. But she really didn't think staying here with Ranger was in her best interest. He looked long and lean in his jeans, reclining on the sofa, and she had been lying anyway about not wanting to kiss him. Jumping his bones would be a sport of choice, but she'd sworn off being a boredom chaser, so now she had to stick to her guns. "I'm ready if you are."

He closed his eyes. "I have a slight headache," he murmured.

"I can drive, if you don't feel well." She leaned forward to peer at him.

A second later, a snore escaped him. Her eyes widened. Dinner in the oven, candles ablaze with romanticism, and he was so bored he'd fallen asleep. This was not a good sign. "Ranger," she whispered. "Ranger! Don't go to sleep on me!"

He didn't move, except for a totally relaxed snore.

"Great." Actually, he had every reason to be exhausted. He'd been very sick, and he hadn't slept comfortably in a few days. "So much for me being your good medicine," she muttered. "More like a sleeping pill."

Still, that left her free to munch on Hawk's dinner. Alone. She grabbed one of the wineglasses from the table, crept into the kitchen and fixed herself a plate full of food. It was a shame that Ranger was missing this wonderful dinner, but maybe it was better if he got his rest.

"Mmm," she said, starting into the casserole. The wine was tasty and velvety, and she sat in the kitchen at the bar, enjoying every bite of her meal. Even the chair was just right, metal, but with a leather seat. She had a perfect view of the outdoors. Dark sky illuminated with diamond lights—there was very little she could think of that would be more romantic than this.

She washed her dishes, holding back a yawn. After she dried them, she went to check on Ranger. He was sleeping comfortably. Obviously, they weren't going anywhere tonight. She might as well rest, too.

Heading back down the small hall, she went into the master bedroom. "Pretty big bed for one person," she murmured, "but I'm sure it'll be just right."

And it was, soft and warm with a heavy comforter. And lonely.

"I need a dog," she told herself. "Maybe a cat."

But not Ranger. Definitely not that bad boy. The last thing she would ever be was his latest toy. He was looking for diversion, and she didn't want to play.

"It's raining," he said suddenly, interrupting her thoughts. She sat straight up in the bed, holding the sheet to her even though she had worn her shirt to bed.

"Raining?"

"Yep. Guess that means we can't try out the hammock on the balcony."

"I wasn't going to, anyway!"

"Are you afraid of storms?" he asked.

She couldn't see him in the darkness, just his silhouette and it made her nervous. She couldn't remember the last time she'd been alone with a man in her sleeping space. "Absolutely not!"

"Good. I didn't want to have to hold you if you got scared."

She scowled in the darkness. "I wouldn't ask you to."

"Glad we got that straightened out. So, the TV says this area is under a tornado watch."

She snorted and pulled a pillow over her head. "A little rain isn't going to do anything but flush out some of the dust."

"I was just testing the honesty of your claim about storms."

"Go away. It's not going to work."

Outside, the rain began to hit the windows.

"Maybe we can't leave until the morning," he said.

"I rather thought that when you began sawing logs on the sofa. I could have left you, but you seemed so trusting and alone that I couldn't. After all, you did give me a ride. Of course, you also brought me into this mess, which I suppose entitles me to ditch you, but I couldn't. We are definitely leaving in the morning, so don't get too comfy on the sofa."

"No room in here?"

"Nope. The bed's too small for two."

"I thought you'd say that. King-size beds have a reputation for being tight. Okay. I'm going to go watch the rain hit the windows."

"You do that," she said, thinking she'd rather he stay in the room with her, but knowing that that way led to disaster.

She could hear his boots head down the hall. To herself, she sighed, thinking she was relieved, and then realizing she was sighing because she couldn't throw back the covers and say, "Bring it on, big boy!"

That made her giggle. "He'd probably have died of shock," she said out loud, enjoying the thought. Except she knew he would have been shocked, but it would have been a good shock. Then he would have dived in with her, and she wouldn't be alone anymore. And it would have felt better than right.

"And now I can't sleep." Thinking about the king-size bed and the rain and the candles was too much temptation. She crept down the hall and peeked around the corner, shamelessly spying.

He stood in front of the window, hands on hips, staring out at the darkness and the rain. Even not moving he seemed very large, very commanding. Her breath caught in her throat. Way sexy, way hot. What was she doing, saying no? What would keeping her distance gain her? She might never have a chance at that much man again! Who cared if she was simply his girl-whirl? She'd be on her riverboat, dealing cards and enjoying the happy memory of one night in a cool hideaway with a major amount of man.

But no, they'd feel awkward around each other in the morning. She was going her way, and he was going his, and she'd be kidding herself if she thought it was just one night of fun between the sheets. She'd started out on this journey to forget about him!

If she slept with him, it would take that much longer to forget about him. In fact, she could develop amnesia and he'd probably be the first thing she'd remember.

''Rats,'' she murmured to herself. The temptation was killing her. ''You know,'' she said to get his attention, ''I hate for you to be bored and scared of storms.''

He turned around, his gaze catching on her with heat. ''I am not bored, and I'm only afraid of hurting you.''

She raised her chin, astonished.

''You're right about us kissing being a bad idea,

but not for the reasons you mentioned. The boredom thing. The truth is, you're delicate and bruised, and I'd like to pound the idiot who hurt your feelings so badly.''

Oh, boy. Her eyes widened. Her throat dried out. She could tell him that actually *he* was the idiot, but obviously he didn't imagine that he'd hurt her. Which made her realize that he had not meant to be careless with her. It was just that the moment she'd met him, she'd known she'd met a man worth having. Only, she wasn't supposed to be falling for a man, and…Ranger wasn't game for love, no matter how sweet he was about wanting to pound someone for her. ''I think you're more man than I can handle,'' she said softly. ''Right now.''

A smile softened his face. ''I think you're a crazy li'l ol' gal. But I could handle you, even though you're kind of a wild thing. I could definitely handle you.''

She pursed her lips. ''Think so?''

''Yeah. And you'd like it. We both would.''

She sucked in a breath. ''Why are you still wearing that ring?''

''*I* like it.''

His eyes warmed her, saw through her. *She* liked it, too. She liked thinking it meant something to him.

''It's my good-luck charm,'' he said. ''Keeps me from falling under the curse.''

''Oh, yeah. Right. I think…I think I'll go back to bed now,'' she said. ''I just thought I should check on you. Make sure you weren't feeling woozy or something.''

''Thanks.''

''Well, goodnight.'' She fled back down to the lonely king-size bed. Whew! Okay, the sooner they hit the road tomorrow, the safer she'd be. She was falling harder, and the feeling was weightless. If she didn't get away from Ranger soon, she was going to be lost.

RANGER LAY ON THE SOFA after blowing out the candles. He'd miscalculated. He'd added up the time he'd spent with Hannah to mean more than it apparently had, and then multiplied it by his lust for her.

But that hadn't equaled getting to hold her in his arms. She liked him; he knew she did. But that wasn't enough for her to get around the fact that he'd kissed Cissy. And, if he was truthful with himself, he would have to admit that Hannah was right: He wasn't in the market for a hot and heavy love affair right now. He had issues, and he respected her for figuring that out. Some women would have slept with him and tried to change his mind, focus his attention on them.

Hannah was different. Even her body language radiated Go away!

Which, perversely, made him want to stay closer to her. Had made him want to marry her in his most weakened moment.

Whew. When he thought that through, he realized how lucky he was not to have made love with her.

He might have started believing his own fairy tale, and then what? Take her back home to the ranch with Mason?

No way. Hannah had no home. She was a gypsy. He couldn't live like that, and he couldn't live with Mason. He was attracted to her because he was bored with his life, as Hannah had pointed out, and her gypsy-ness called to him.

But in the end, it wouldn't work out. They'd have great sex and nothing else.

Of course, great sex was worth considering.

But…not with Hannah. She was already too emotionally pained. He wondered who had hurt her. He wondered why men did that to women.

He sank onto the sofa and wondered why women did that to men. Why wasn't love easy?

With a start, he realized Hannah was standing in front of him. With the wind and rain wildly hitting the windows, he hadn't heard her walk into the room. He gazed up at her face, soft and sweet in the darkness, her eyes huge and wary like a squirrel's. ''Hey,'' he said softly. ''Can't sleep?''

He thought she trembled. ''I don't think I can,'' she said.

''Storm bugging you?''

She shook her head. ''You're bugging me.''

He stared at her for a moment, adding the tremble and her words correctly. She'd changed her mind about making love with him. The realization made his blood pound in his head, made his pulse strong with desire.

But…he'd never know why she'd done it. They were too far from the real world for it to count. Sex was sex and his brothers would say he was weird for not jerking her down onto the floor with him and losing himself in her all night.

But there was more to life than quickies. Tomorrow he would be glad he hadn't taken advantage of her.

"Come here," he said, pulling her down in front of him so that they lay spoon-style on the sofa. He buried his face in her shoulder so he could smell her neck and her hair, and put his arm around her waist to anchor her safely to him. Now, let it storm all it wants. I've got Miss Funky-Punky in my arms.

Chapter Seven

Hannah sighed to herself as she melted into Ranger's arms. It had taken all her courage to come back down the hall to him, wanting him and yet not wanting him. Wanting something more than what they'd had so far, knowing she didn't have any more than this to offer him.

And maybe he understood that she was just lonely. That's all it was. She was lonely and scared of her life. It was going nowhere, and she had as many issues as he did, only she wasn't admitting it. It would be heaven to make love with him, but tomorrow she would be glad she didn't take advantage of him.

She closed her eyes. It felt great to be curled up against Ranger, even if she knew it was only for one night.

Tomorrow, she had to get to Mississippi.

Ranger had to offer himself to the military.

"I'm thirty-six," she whispered to Ranger. "Just in case you thought I looked too young for you."

"I'm thirty-two," he whispered back, "just in case you thought I looked too old for you."

"Do you really think the military will take you?"

"Yeah. I'm strong and willing and possessed of all my faculties and at least I can swab decks or something. Do you really think the riverboat will let you deal cards to ogling men?"

"Yes. I'm smart and willing and possessed of all my faculties and really good at it. Besides, the man I was supposed to marry owns the boat."

Ranger sat up and flipped on the lamp beside the table, pulling her to sit beside him. "Okay," he said, "you can't slip that humdinger in there like it doesn't count. You married me under false pretenses."

"I didn't really marry you. It was the fakest of fake marriages. And I'm not married to him. I said I was supposed to marry him. Why are you so outraged?"

"Because I'm going into the military where there are no women, or at least not many, and you're going to a riverboat that a significant other of yours owns," he said, feeling huffy.

"The two have no relation."

"Hannah Hotchkiss," Ranger said, his voice intense, "you're making up a phantom man to keep your distance from me, aren't you? A cardboard fiancé?"

"No. Truly, you're safe from me."

"Damn right I am! Because I wouldn't touch a woman who had a boyfriend, and you know it. Don't you?"

"Yes, I do. But that has nothing to do with anything."

He stood. "It has everything to do with everything. Is that the joker who stomped on your heart and made you so nontrusting? You definitely have trust issues."

"No," she said emphatically. "And that's not my issue, thank you."

"It was someone else?"

"Yes."

"Go back to bed," he said.

"Ranger!"

"Go back to bed. There's only room for one on this sofa, and that one is going to be me. I'll be up at first light to get you on the road toward Mississippi."

"Fine." She got up from the sofa and flounced down the hall.

"Fine," he mimicked.

"Fine," he said again. His every cell seemed to have closed up inside him, gasping with shock. The man she was supposed to marry! What the hell kind of bomb was that to drop on a man who still had some lingering cactus needles lodged in his feet? They were small and spiny and they bothered him— he'd need tweezers and a strong light to get them out and maybe a real doctor—but they were nothing like the strange, cracking feeling inside him right now.

It was the Curse of the Broken Body Parts, and it was massacring his heart. He had to break the curse—*fast*.

"CHANGE OF PLAN," Ranger said to Hannah the next morning. He'd gone into the bedroom and found her sitting up, wide-eyed and wild-haired and too cute for his own good. "Out of the sack, sweetie. I'm going to feed you some breakfast and some coffee, and then we're borrowing Hawk's truck and we're heading for that riverboat of yours."

Her lips parted, something he found disturbingly attractive. "What about the military?"

"This minor detour won't take long. I can't allow you to travel alone. Too much befalls you. You're not really safe to the general public. So I'm appointing myself your bodyguard, to protect everyone involved."

Her eyes narrowed slightly as she pulled the sheet up to her chin over her crossed legs. "I think you have something wrong there. Too much befalls *you*. I don't need you, Ranger. I got along fine without you for thirty-six years."

"See, but that's just it. I don't think you *have* gotten along fine without me. You need assistance, and I'm free."

"You want to see the man I was supposed to marry. Because you don't believe he exists."

He raised a sardonic brow. "Methinks you are one to invent tales, my dear, but I don't hold that against you. Really. It matters not a bit to me if you author the next bestseller on manhunting. I will deliver you to your significant other safe and sound, take a spin on your riverboat, assure myself of your safety and then be off. This is what friends do for each other."

"He is not my significant other. He was going to be, but then I changed my mind. And you and I are not friends," she reminded him.

"I figured you for a fickle female. I do feel for the poor chap you changed your mind on."

"Yesterday you wanted to pound some man on my beha—"

"And as for friends, you and I are on pecking terms," he insisted. "That stands for something. My father felt strongly about chivalry. He also felt that a man often wants what he can't have, and sometimes not to his betterment."

She cocked her head at him. "What illustration are you making? That you want me but it's really better if you don't have me?"

He backed away from the door, grinning. "Breakfast in thirty minutes. Pack your bag. We're hitting the road to Mississippi."

"What about Hawk's truck?" she called after him.

"I'll return it safe and sound, just as he better do to mine," Ranger called back. "Dress quickly. The sooner we get there, the better."

HANNAH STARED AFTER RANGER. The man had lost it. He was acting strangely, but then he and all his brothers were devilishly enigmatic. There was all this unrealized sexual tension between her and Ranger which could be factored in, but his new desire to enter her world and see her riverboat and the man she was supposed to have married was puzzling.

And when he met the man he'd called her "significant other," he was going to be in for a shock.

She hoped it was one he took well.

"MASON," MIMI CALLED as she tapped on the front door of his house, opening it to stick her head inside. "Mason, it's me!"

"In the kitchen," he called back. "Hey, Mimi. You really look nice."

What she would have given for him to have told her that before! "Thanks. So do you."

"I'm heading out to a party. Have to put on a bolo for that, I guess. And clean jeans."

She knew he was referring to the party that the new gals in town were having tonight, in the home above their hair salon. A momentary flicker of jealousy hit her, but she pushed that aside. There was no place for those feelings in her life anymore.

"You and Brian going?"

"No. I've got to finish packing. And I'm getting nervous about leaving."

He frowned. "Flying bother you?"

"No. I'm worried about leaving Dad."

"Shoot. Mimi, the sheriff'll outlive us all. He can take care of himself fine."

She sat in a kitchen chair, wondering how much to

tell Mason. After all, they were neighbors. Once best friends. Her dad shouldn't mind her talking to Mason—but then again, he was the sheriff. If he was going to make a one-way trip to the ranch in the sky, he was going to do it without a lot of people fussing over him. And without folks thinking they could use his weakened condition to break the law. "Mason," she said softly, "he's my dad. All I've got besides Brian."

"Mimi, honey." He sat down next to her. "What's gotten into you?"

Shaking her head, she didn't allow the tears of worry to push past her eyes. "I really need to know that you'll look in on him. Often."

"You know I'll do whatever you want." He took her hand in his. "And I can have my ornery brothers check on him, too."

"No! Only you. Please." She could trust Mason to do as he said. And maybe Last. But she didn't want Last to figure out her secret. And he would. Mason was the most responsible of the lot, and he was also the most likely to overlook telling details.

Last was so sensitive he'd figure everything out in a second. And then her father would be upset and embarrassed.

"I really need to go on this honeymoon," she told Mason, making certain her voice carried her urgency. "But I need to know that you'll do everything as I say. No deviation from the plan."

He grinned at her. "Mimi, we've always deviated from any plan we ever had."

"Not this time, Mason." She took a deep breath. "And here's the phone number to the hotel, in case you need to call me."

He looked at the paper as if it might burst into flames any second. "Uh, Mimi, I'm not going to call you on your honeymoo—"

"Mason! Please!"

"Hey. Hey, little gal, slow down and relax." He released her hand and leaned back to take a good look at her. "Is there something you want to talk about?"

"No." She shook her head, wiping the back of her hand across her eyes.

"Everything okay with you and Brian, right?"

"Everything's fine." She nodded emphatically. "And it'll be even better. Soon."

"Okay, then. You just let me take care of the sheriff."

She smiled at his confidence. He really was making her feel better. "I knew I could count on you. I'll pay you back somehow. Someday."

He raised his brows. "Actually, you could now."

This was more like Mason of old, the teasing in his voice, the grin in his eyes. How she'd missed that! "I don't have time for plots. I've got to finish packing."

"I need to know something. Just a little piece of info is all I want."

"Okay. I'll give it to you if I can." Her heart

heated and stirred inside her, those feelings she thought she'd put to rest once and for all. But she and Mason had always had the most fun when something messy was cooking between them.

"My brothers tattled on you about Helga."

Uh-oh. This was trouble she hadn't expected. "Tattled on me about Helga?" she repeated to buy time.

"They said she wasn't the one who hung the curtains and kept this place together after the flood."

"Well, I really don't know, Mason. It wasn't me."

He looked at her, his gaze gleaming and mischievous. "They say Annabelle did all the work, but that you didn't like her."

"I like Annabelle just fine!"

"Now. But not then. You told your friend, Julia Finehurst of the Honey-Do Agency, that you wanted a battle-ax sent out to work here."

Her eyes shifted of their own accord. "Well, maybe I said I thought you should have someone *mature* in the house. After all, you wouldn't want some young thing distracting your brothers, would you? And goodness, a young girl's reputation has to be thought of. Helga's more of a mother figure, a chaperone to you men. Something to soften the Malfunction Junction wild-man image. Don't you think?"

"Mimi." He drummed the table for an instant. "You did trick me."

"No, I did what I told you I was going to do in the beginning. Remember the e-mail we wrote? I definitely said an older woman was preferred."

"But after Annabelle was here, you let me think Helga had made all the changes."

"You could have asked, Mason. Really."

"I think you believe that I overlook details, Mimi."

She couldn't help her gaze widening innocently. "You may be just a little absentminded, Mason. Details have a way of getting past you."

"And I did miss that Helga doesn't do much except boss my brothers like a termagant."

"A what, Mason?" She frowned. "Have you picked up a new word?"

"It's the word Bandera used to describe Helga. It means a shrew, Mimi," he said softly. "My brothers are leaving the ranch to get away from her. You told me that a housekeeper would keep things tidy. Make things better. But it's made things worse. And you let it stay that way because you preferred a Helga to an Annabelle."

She pursed her lips at him. "They're grown men, Mason. They can get used to a housekeeper who wants them to keep their boots off the table. I don't think they're leaving because of Helga, but you can believe that if you want." Standing, she put her hands on her hips. "Is there any other burning issue you'd like the answer to?"

"There is, actually. Why do *you* think they're leaving?"

Nobody wanted to have this talk with Mason. It was a circular conversation, because he believed what he wanted to believe. He did what he wanted to do, and the consequences be damned. But he was asking for the truth, and by golly, she didn't mind giving it to him, if for no other reason than to take a little pain out of her own scar tissue—courtesy of the hard-headed man standing in front of her. "Because you take all your frustration out on them, Mason. That's why they're wild. That's why they're leaving. Once Frisco Joe opened the gate, they saw freedom just outside their fences. And so they're going, one way or the other."

He crossed his arms and stared at her. "I think Helga's why they're leaving."

"And I think it's you. But we've never agreed on much, Mason, which is why we liked hanging around each other. You steadied me, and I unsteadied you."

"What if I fire Helga?"

"Go right ahead. Cut yourself out of a good house-keeper who's not afraid of your moods."

"My moods!"

"Yes," she said defiantly. "And when you're ready for me to tell you why you're such a horse's ass, I'll be happy to do that, too. Because I'm the only one who will."

He stood, too, towering above her, but she held herself tall and glared back.

"My brothers think you liked knowing I wouldn't be looking around for a woman if all my shopping, my cooking, my washing and my cleaning was taken

care of. And they say you sicced Helga on us out of
spite because I didn't ask you to marry me.''

"Get over it," she snapped. "I have."

And she walked out the front door, giving it a good
slam because she felt like venting right here at his
house, where a good vent would feel the best.

What a horse's ass. She would never admit that
she'd wanted to marry him. Never. That had been her
secret all these years—blast his brothers for trying to
save their own skins—and it was a secret she'd be
keeping.

Among others.

At this point, her life required secrets. And no one,
not even Mason, would know them.

MASON SQUINTED his eyes when Mimi slammed the
door, his ears ringing. That hadn't gone the way he'd
meant it to, but with Mimi, nothing was easy.

She had wanted to marry him, the little torturer.
And he'd been a brainless ox not to see that she'd
wanted him that way. His heart expanded. It felt like
a golden chalice inside him, won at the end of a long,
wearing quest.

And yet, while it made him feel good, it also made
him feel worse. She would never be his.

"Hey," Tex said, slapping Mason on the back as
he walked into the kitchen. "Heard from the rene-
gades? Archer and Ranger?"

"No." Mason rubbed his chin, thinking. Mimi

claimed his brothers were deserting because of him. But she was wrong. "I may fire Helga."

"You do that," Tex said cheerfully on his way to grab some orange juice out of the fridge. "Don't let me slow you down. One more reason to celebrate tonight. Party, party!" He hesitated, then turned. "Why now?"

"Just because," Mason said, testing the water.

"Oh. Hey, are you all right? I smell...perfume." Tex sniffed the air again.

"Mimi was just here."

Tex stared at him. "And does she know you're planning to get rid of her auto-bot? She'll allow it?"

Mason's teeth ground together. "Helga is not an auto-bot. And Mimi doesn't do the hiring and firing around here. I do. With input from all of you, I might add."

"We've been inputting for weeks. It hasn't helped. Where are you going all duded up?"

"To the party. Aren't you going?"

"Yeah. In a bit." Tex winked at him. "Maybe you oughta ask out one of those new gals. Nothing like a new woman to get you over an old woman."

"I don't need to get over Mimi," Mason asserted as haughtily as he could.

Tex laughed and took the orange juice with him. "I was speaking of Helga," he called over his shoulder. "Old woman? Get it? The one you're supposedly firing."

"Shh!" Mason hissed, in case Helga was around,

and she did tend to stay quite close to him. Up till now he'd liked that about her; he'd liked having his every beck and call immediately answered. But now that he knew Helga was a plant sent by Mimi, one of her twisted ideas, he wasn't amused.

"Very funny, Tex," he muttered. But his thoughts wandered back to Mimi. He wasn't surprised that she'd pulled a fast one on him. She'd done that constantly. In fact, he reluctantly admitted missing her hijinks.

But there was nothing he could do about that now.

"You know, Mason," Tex said, poking his head back into the kitchen, "that new woman idea is probably worth thinking over. A woman is probably just what you need. Not necessarily new or old. Just…a woman."

"How about you mind your own business, Dr. Love?" Mason demanded.

Tex disappeared from the doorway. Mason looked out the window toward the Cannadys'. Mimi was leaving, driving Brian's sports car. Even at a distance, he could see that it was her—and that she was driving fast.

Big hurry to get on that honeymoon.

"Maybe I *should* start dating," he told himself. "Just a date every once in a while." To prove he wasn't as much of a horse's ass as Mimi claimed.

Yeah. That was it.

He would date. He needed a woman. Not that he

wasn't happy for her, but he was playing Keep Away from Mimi with his thoughts, and his brain was racking up the win so far.

He definitely needed a woman.

Chapter Eight

"I've got the map out," Hannah told Ranger as she dug around in the console of Hawk's truck. "So we don't take any more detours."

"Burn the map," Ranger said. "You and I are taking the long way to the river."

"The long way?" She looked at her impatient driver. "I thought you said we were in a hurry to get there."

"I was primarily focused on getting out of Hawk's lair. There was far too much romance, and you weren't succumbing to that. I don't think you trust me. Maybe men in general."

She snapped the console closed after replacing the map. "I think Hawk is pretty sneaky. No guy has all that romantic stuff like candles and bubble bath unless he's expecting company. And then he left it all behind like it was nothing. Like he didn't expect female company any time soon. I think he does all that medicine man stuff to lure females."

"Hey, don't knock it. Every man's got his game.

But don't start obsessing about him. He could be married and his missus left him, for all we know.''

Hannah considered that. ''He said he was going to track someone. That's kind of an unusual statement to make, don't you think?''

''I think he's an unusual guy. And I'll be forever grateful to him for saving me since Archer obviously wasn't going to. Or you, for that matter.''

She looked out a window. ''When you told me that piece of advice of your father's, were you…I mean, you sort of sounded like he wasn't around anymore.''

''He's not.''

''Oh. I'm sorry.'' She'd been afraid of that.

''Far as I know, he's not dead. He's just not around. Or he could be dead. I don't know.''

Ranger's voice was terse. Hannah turned to look at him. ''For a long time?''

''Since the day Mason turned seventeen. We never knew where Maverick went. He just went away, leaving a note behind that said he…he loved us, he would miss us, but he just couldn't go on living without our mother. And that he knew we'd be fine.'' Ranger took a deep breath. ''And then Mason was on his own raising us, just like Maverick was on his own at seventeen.''

''And you've never gotten a phone call from him? A letter?''

He shook his head. ''Not so much as a postcard. And yes, we filed a missing persons report. We sent out letters to anyone we thought who might know something. He simply disappeared, him and his broken heart. The fact is, we were lucky Mason was able to keep us all together. There were a lot of folks in town who said we belonged in foster care. In fact, there's a lot of folks who still believe the state shouldn't have left us with Mason.'' He shrugged. ''They couldn't have stopped us. We would have set everything in the town on fire before we allowed them to separate us.''

''Ranger!'' Hannah was surprised but not shocked—and her heart was torn over the raw emotion in his voice.

''In the end, we did what we wanted. And they call our ranch Malfunction Junction because we used to get into a little trouble. Not enough to get arrested— well, maybe, if Sheriff Cannady hadn't been next door to bust our heads instead of hauling us to the county jail every once in a while. Mrs. Cannady used to cook for us some, but then she up and left for the bright lights of Hollywood, and that was the last anyone heard of her. Believe me, nobody even dares mention Mrs. Cannady around Mimi. Once that ugly genie is out of the verbal bottle, it's like watching our little sister turn into a she-devil on command.'' He glanced at Hannah. ''It's not pretty.''

''Poor Mimi!''

''Yeah. She's had it rough. We would have felt pretty sorry for ourselves if it hadn't been for Mimi. She kept the pity party to a dull roar. At least we know why our dad left. His heart was broken, and he kind of lost it. We knew he was losing his grip. But Mrs. Cannady just left because she felt like it, and she abandoned a daughter and a husband who didn't deserve to be dumped.''

''Maybe Hawk could track your dad,'' Hannah suggested absently as she dug some pretzels out of a bag for Ranger.

''I could track him myself at this point, I guess. Or any of us could go looking for him, though I'm not sure where we'd start. But we came to the conclusion that if he wanted to be found, he would have let us know.''

He munched some of the pretzels she handed him. ''You're not so bad when you're not trying to romance me,'' she said.

''Yeah, well. I still fantasize about winning your shirt. I mean, what man wouldn't?'' His gaze skimmed over her before returning to the road.

''That's kind of sweet, in a boneheaded sort of way.'' She popped the tops on some Big Reds and placed them in the cup holders. ''I've always been on my own.''

''Tell me something hard to figure out.''

''I wanted to say yes to you about the romantic interlude. But I got scared.''

He turned to cock a brow at her. ''You should be scared.''

''I know. I am. I mean, how can I want a man who just wants to use me to chase off his boredom?''

"Well, it's not only that. You're cute, for a whacky girl. You disturb me. In a good sort of way."

"But it would be better if you didn't have me. That's what you think your father's advice meant."

"No. I think sometimes things are not meant to be. And you are definitely not in the plans, obviously. But that doesn't mean it's a good thing or a bad thing. You're just meant to remain an unknown in my life."

"I thought men lusted after unknowns. Strived for them."

"They do. But their common sense kicks in, too. It tells them some things are unknown and gonna stay that way, so head to a greener pasture."

"Like you did with Cissy." She nodded sagely.

"Look. You've got that a little skewed. Cissy is a nice girl, and what guy wouldn't want to kiss her—"

"She's about ten years younger than me."

"Oh." Ranger gave her a sidelong glance. "Don't give me that innocent look. Now I know what the problem was all along. Hannah Hotchkiss, you're pouting!"

"What?"

"You're feeling sorry for yourself because you're the older woman!" And he started roaring with laughter.

She started to say something to shut him up, to put him firmly in his place, but then changed her mind, popping another pretzel into her mouth instead.

And then she smiled.

RANGER DIDN'T LIKE IT when Hannah smiled like that. She was keeping a secret, and that wasn't a good sign. Especially when he was supposed to have been winning their verbal volley. "Listen, maybe the riverboat isn't a good idea for you."

"Why not?"

She opened her eyes, big and innocent, and he gathered himself up to do more verbal battle. "You're too delicate. Far too innocent," he said importantly. "It sounds very dangerous to be an unchaperoned female on a boat where men will be, carousing and…and other things."

Her stare had a twinkle in it. He pursed his lips and set the cruise control.

"Have you appointed yourself my guardian?"

"I told you we think of you as someone special," he said gruffly.

"We?"

"And I just want to see you safe. Out of harm's way. So naturally I'm concerned about you gallivanting off on a riverboat."

"Maybe you should come with me," she suggested.

His brows rose. The thought had occurred to him, but he wouldn't have dreamed of suggesting it. He'd been hoping for an invitation, but now that he had it, he wanted to make certain her suggestion was sincere. "I think the military might be an easier assignment than watching a woman on a riverboat."

"I didn't say come and be my bodyguard," Hannah said with a laugh. "Come watch me play."

"Play?"

"Deal the cards."

"Oh. And play the suckers."

She frowned. "The casino doesn't take bets for less than five thousand dollars."

He whistled. "That doesn't allow for suckers."

"No, it doesn't. Anyway, that's why I invited you to come watch me."

He thought about that. "You're suggesting I don't have the wherewithal for such a game?"

"I'm saying there's no point in you losing that much money. Especially to act as if you're keeping an eye on me, which I don't need, by the way."

Ranger was outraged. "First, how do you know I would lose?"

She shrugged. "Your face gives away every thought you're having."

"It does?" That disgruntled him. It'd be a lot healthier for him emotionally if this wiry-haired female couldn't read his face.

"Pretty much. I know that right now you're feeling testy about what I said. A few moments before that, you were thinking guardian thoughts, but not necessarily those of a brother."

"How do you know that?"

She smiled at him. "Because you looked at my legs when you said that it might not be safe at the casino."

He forced his eyes back to the road where she

couldn't read them. But bingo, she had him. The thoughts he was having were more of the possessive type. And for what? She'd thrown his ring in the dirt. He'd rather set his own hay bales on fire than admit she'd damaged his pride. In his pocket was the ring he'd scooped from the dirt, after she'd turned her back. He'd hoped to adopt a careless attitude about it, but it didn't seem to be getting through to his head.

"And there are very thick layers inside your head," she said.

He jerked around to stare at her.

"Very thick skull," she clarified. "You'd best keep your eyes on the road, cowboy."

"How did you know what I was thinking?" he demanded. "And for the record, my thick skull was a boon in rodeoing."

She smiled sublimely. "I didn't know what you were thinking. I was talking about gambling. You don't have a poker face, and you have a very thick skull. Gamblers are usually more easygoing, at least on the outside." Her smile grew broader. "You're always tense."

"You make me that way!"

She tapped him on the arm. "You make yourself tense. I don't think the military will want you. No poker face, no easy spirit. You should get married, Ranger."

His jaw went slack for a moment. "How would that help?"

"It would relax you, for starters."

"You don't relax me."

"Yes, but we're not married."

"Even when we were, you didn't relax me."

"I inoculated you from the phobia of bad luck, though. You said so yourself. The Curse of the Broken Body Parts? Remember?"

He didn't want to talk about that, so he declined to answer.

"You became immune to your hypochondria when you married me. So marriage is good for you. Not to me, because I don't want to be married. But marriage to someone."

"Just about the only other single woman I know is Cissy," he said sneakily.

"I don't think so," Hannah replied without looking at him. "She's in love with someone else. Plus she's married, so that's a problem for that plan."

"Whoa. Hang on there. Cissy is married?"

"Yeah. That's one of the reasons she's traveling with me. Her husband up and disappeared two years ago, and she fell in with Marvella for employment. She's got some younger siblings she supports. But she wanted to have a different life than she can have with Marvella, so I invited her to my ex-fiancé's riverboat."

Ranger felt his teeth go on edge. All this talk of ex-fiancé's and disappearing husbands was enough to make him nervous. "I don't understand how she's married but in love with someone else. Not that I should be saying this, but Tex had a major itch going for her last month at the rodeo.''

''He did?''

''Yeah. But she's too elegant for Malfunction Junction. Anyway, what about the disappearing husband?''

''Well, apparently, the police told Cissy that her husband was involved in some illegal matters that he never bothered to share with her. Had Cissy known, she would have given him the very hard boot. Remember, she had siblings to support. She didn't need any bad examples in their lives. But she didn't know any of this until he came up missing.'' Hannah sighed. ''The police think they'll only find his body if they ever do find him.''

''Wow. That was some unsavory stuff he must have been involved in.''

She nodded. ''Drugs. Dealing, mostly. But he told Cissy that his family was privately wealthy and that he'd take care of her nine siblings if she married him. He wanted a wife for respectability, because the stakes were high, I guess. But it all turned out badly, and Cissy says she's never marrying for convenience again. And certainly not for money.''

''Marriage of convenience?'' Ranger asked slowly. ''As in, they never…''

She shook her head. ''Never. So now she's looking for a new job, a new way of life. Her mother is wheelchair-bound, but has been watching the kids while Cissy worked for Marvella.''

"And now on your riverboat."

"It's not my riverboat."

"I don't know. I don't think I like it. You were safer with Delilah."

She cocked her head at him. "Have you already appointed yourself my bodyguard?"

He shrugged that off with a frown. "How long are you planning on staying on this job? I might point out that you seem to be a bit flighty."

"This from a man who rolls down a hill nearly nude."

He gave her a stern look. "We've talked about my family, we've talked about Cissy. It seems to me that we talk about everything except you, Hannah Hotchkiss." He turned back to look at the road but his mind was working hard. "Did you deliberately occupy my brain so I wouldn't ask anything personal about you?"

"No. Your brain appears to be permanently vacant."

Okay. He'd set himself up for that. "Wisenheimer, could you please fill me in on your life?"

"Is that why you're taking the scenic route? And driving thirty miles an hour? I could get there faster if I walked."

"I couldn't. I think I've still got some needles in my feet."

"Do you want me to drive?"

He shook his head. "You talk. And keep me awake."

"Didn't you sleep well last night?"

Not with her sleeping down the hall. All he could think about was her warm body under the covers. "Don't deviate from your assignment."

"My life story won't keep you awake. It's not as interesting as yours. In fact, it's downright boring. Let's choose another subject."

"Hannah, I'm a captive audience. Try out my attention span."

She shifted in the seat next to him. "What do you want to know?"

Everything. "Why do you wear toeless tennis shoes?"

"They're different."

He digested that. "Why do you color your hair that way?"

"I like to be different. Do you like it?"

He nodded. "Surprisingly, I do. It suits you. So, do you mind me asking about your folks?"

"They're…different," she murmured.

"I know, everything about you is different. So tell me."

"They're faith healers, for starters. And hippies, for the big finish."

His brows went up. "You sound as if you disapprove." He couldn't resist a peek at her expression, which was very unhappy.

"As a child, I wasn't allowed to see doctors." She shrugged. "I developed a medical condition in my late teens involving my female organs. My parents felt everything could be healed with prayer, and that I must not be praying hard enough. Believing hard enough. Being good enough. In the end, I couldn't take it anymore. I left home; I went to several doctors, who all agreed there was nothing to do but remove everything that was ruining my life. For me, that also included my parents.''

"Hannah—"

She shook her head. "It's fine now. I had the surgery, and I started living my life over. Not with my parents, of course. I couldn't survive in their world."

His lips compressed. "I'm so sorry."

"I'd like to say it's okay, but it wasn't. I was the only child, so one day…I think I'll have to go home and forgive them. I'm just not ready to. I call them every once in a while. But our worlds are just too different, and I can't have children, so we don't have much reason to forge a future. Except that they're my parents…''

He was sorry he'd made her talk about it. "I shouldn't have asked. Let me change the subject."

"It's all right. You told me about your father." She patted his arm, and her hand lingered for a second before moving away. "You're the only person I've ever told about my parents, except for my almost-fiancé."

Instantly, he couldn't help worrying that this ex-boyfriend meant more to her than she was letting on. And then he told himself not to be so insecure. He should be glad she'd had someone to lean on.

He wanted it to be him. "Hannah, I wish I'd known you then."

"No, you don't. I'm just now settling down. I've been a rebel all my life."

"And you don't want to get married."

She shook her head. "I really can see no purpose in it for me."

"But you like me."

The smile she gave him melted his heart. "I do, cowboy. Sort of. Keep your eyes on the road."

"Okay, so I'll just come with you for a while and amuse myself on the riverboat. And protect you from leches."

"And when you get bored?" she softly asked. "Because you will. You're not suited for just hanging around."

"I'll jump overboard and swim back to shore. Then head for the military."

"Just a break in your action?"

He matched her light, airy tone with a shrug. "Sure. Why not? It's great weather. You're fun. You beat me at strip poker."

"Ah. You associate me with diverse things."

"I associate you with weirdness. But that doesn't mean I'm going to marry you again, so keep it cool, wild thing." He kept his tone light in a desperate bid to be smooth.

She nodded. "No marriage."

"No broken body parts. Just fun."

"That's right. Something different."

And then Ranger stopped the truck. "I've driven so many back roads that I've lost my sense of direction."

Hannah cocked a brow at him and put the window down, sticking a bare foot out into the breezy air as she reclined. "I'll figure out the map if you crack me a soda."

"You'll figure out the map?"

"You got us lost. Should I trust you further? I do have a boat to catch," she pointed out. "He leaves tomorrow."

Ranger's head swiveled so he could stare at her full-on. Big brown eyes meeting inquisitive ones. "Why didn't you mention that before?"

"It wasn't important. Was it?"

It was important to Ranger. They were lost. They could stay lost. The riverboat could leave without them. More importantly, the boyfriend could sail off without Hannah.

Her eyes were luminous as she tried to outthink him. But he worked on that poker face, keeping his dishonorable thoughts to himself. When they'd left Lonely Hearts Station, he'd kept an eye on her in the rearview mirror while she frolicked in the back seat with Archer. Even then, he'd itched to know more about her. His gaze wanted to be on her every second.

What he was thinking now was tantamount to…well, girlnapping, he told himself sternly. It would be like days of old, where the scoundrel took his young maiden at will.

They'd both agreed to have fun with each other. Nothing deep, nothing dangerous. But something about this girl made him think like a caveman. He *had* married her in a cave....

But he wanted her in this truck—or, actually, anywhere he could have her.

"Ranger," Hannah said thoughtfully, "you have suddenly developed a damned convincing poker face."

Chapter Nine

"And we both like it that way," Ranger said. "Don't we?"

"I'm not sure." Hannah stared at the new Ranger evolving in front of her. "I think you're scaring me. I like the you I could figure out. Bring him back at once and never go schizo on me again."

He laughed at her, tugging at her hair. "Now, Hannah, you are the elder in this truck. You are the card dealer who can figure out her customers at a glance. Surely you have this all figured out."

And then he pulled her into his arms, kissing her as if her lips were his final destination in life. She groaned, leaning into him to get closer. Her lips seemed to have a life of their own; her body wanted to go places she would have denied herself. Warmth spread over her, turning to sizzling heat. "More," she gasped when he pulled back for a moment to stare into her eyes. "Don't stop. I haven't been kissed like that before, cowboy. I want my eight minutes in the saddle."

''Seconds,'' he corrected, his gaze amused.

''I want *minutes*.''

He laughed and pushed her gently back into the seat. ''Hannah, I think we should change your last name.''

Already miffed that he was acting so nonchalantly about a kiss that had set her on fire, she retorted, ''I thought we agreed no marriage.''

''Oh, we did. I'm only suggesting that maybe you should change your last name to HotKiss. Hannah HotKiss has a certain *ring* to it, don't you think?''

Her jaw dropped at his flippancy. She wanted to push him down a hill herself. He was *teasing* her— and it only served to sharpen her sexual attraction to him! His eyes gleamed, no longer hiding his thoughts, and she saw that he knew he'd turned her on with a vengeance.

''I want to call you a bad word with a French pronunciation, but I'll restrict myself to helping you find the proper road,'' she said, reaching for the map.

The sun was going down, and the truck was getting warm. Or she had gotten hot.

He took the map from her and dangled it outside the window, before reaching into the console with his free hand.

''What are you doing?'' she asked suspiciously, her blood starting to thunder with a little nervousness, a bit of trepidation and a lot of wet, hot desire.

''Lighting you a fire.'' He took out a lighter and

set fire to the map, which flamed up faster than a girl could pucker her lips. "It gets *real* cold around here at night."

ON THE RIVERBOAT, Cissy anxiously watched the road leading to the dock. "Maybe we should call them," she said to Archer. "They should have been here by now. Shouldn't they?"

Archer sighed. "Could you let it go? They're fine. Why aren't you worried about Hawk? We dropped him off in a roadside forest near a small town with a name I can't remember, so he could track something. Why can't he be a normal male—get dropped off in a bar to track women?"

"That's your idea of normal?"

Archer shook his head and went back to the issue they were really arguing about. "Ranger and Hannah would have called us if they were stuck. Maybe they stopped to look at landmarks."

Cissy's eyebrows went up. "Landmarks? I don't think so. Hannah was in a hurry to be on the river. Said she had some things she needed to think about. Or, not think about."

Archer crossed his legs and leaned into the rail. "Chiefly my brother, right?"

"Girls never tell on their gal pals. Don't ask me."

He laughed. "She digs my brother. I could tell."

"*Digging* is not an appropriate word for a woman's feelings," Cissy said primly.

He laughed again.

"Let's call them." She scanned the road again. "Jellyfish said we're leaving at nightfall."

"I still can't believe his name is Jellyfish. And Hannah nearly married him."

"There are reasons for everything," Cissy told him sternly. "And not always those that the male pea-brain can comprehend."

Archer shook his head and squinted his eyes with concentration. "We're in Mississippi. There are no jellyfish here. Explain that to this country boy, because where I come from, we call a man what he is. And if his name is Jellyfish, well, that indicates a problem."

Cissy giggled. "All your Texas tough talk, a-spade-is-a-spade stuff. His name is Jellyfish. That's what it is. Get over it."

"Hawk. Jellyfish. I feel like I'm stuck in a cross between 'Wild Kingdom' and *The Crocodile Hunter.* Can't they have normal names?" He scowled.

Cissy lasered a stare on him. "Oh, yeah. Well, it's so much better to be named after towns or states. Like, if your brother ever gets amnesia, when he comes to and they want to know his name he can just say, what state is this? And they'll say Texas. And he can say, 'Dude! That's it! I'm Texas from Texas!'" She turned her head to scan the road leading to the dock.

"You think about him a lot, don't you?"

"Mind your own business."

"Hey. Did you talk to your customers like that?

Because if you did, I'm amazed that any returned at all.''

Cissy was feeling very snippy, and it had to do with Tex. And she didn't want to be teased about it. Her half-hearted playfulness gave way to a defensive shield. ''This from a man who's so conversationally stunted he has to have an e-mail relationship with a gal in Australia. For all you know, Archer, it was a guy you were corresponding with for all those months.''

His jaw dropped. ''A guy!''

''Yes, a guy,'' she mimicked. ''Now either you call and check on my friend, or I'm going to push you overboard and leave you without a paddle.''

Archer was disgruntled, but he pulled the cell phone from his pocket. ''I still think we shouldn't bother them. Ranger knows what he's doing.''

She sighed. ''I know. It's a Jefferson thing, to know what he's doing. Right. Dial.''

''Here, you talk.''

Cissy snatched the phone from him impatiently. Really! If he weren't Tex's brother, she'd be inclined to stomp his boot. They were all hardheaded men— and maybe unattractively so! ''Hello? Hannah?''

She listened for a moment to the garble on the other end. ''What? The map's on fire? Where are you? What do you mean, you don't know? It was a straight shot from Hawk's place! We can come get you—''

Slowly, she pulled the cell phone away from her ear. Turning it off, she handed it back to Archer, who was staring at her quizzically. "They won't be making the riverboat," she said. "Ranger's got them so lost they don't know where they are."

Archer laughed out loud. "Good old Ranger," he said.

Cissy rolled her eyes and went to find Jellyfish.

AT MALFUNCTION JUNCTION, Mason headed over to check on Sheriff Cannady. Although, truth be known, the sheriff ought to be checking on him. Mimi's father was one of the fittest men he'd ever known—once, he'd seen him take down two beefy brawlers, one in each arm, knocking their heads before tying their feet together, heel-to-heel. The sheriff was a tough guy. Mimi might have a tender heart, but she had her daddy's nerves of steel, that was for certain.

No one answered his knock, so he opened the front door and peered in. "Sheriff?" he called. "It's Mason."

There was no reply. And yet, he'd seen the sheriff's truck out back in its customary spot. "Ah, sheriff," he called from the base of the stairwell.

He thought he heard a muted reply from upstairs. Frowning, he said, "I'm coming up, sheriff."

Slowly, he headed up, giving the man a chance to dress if necessary. It was going to be plain embarrassing if the man had company and Mason had butted in like a greenhorn. And yet, his promise to Mimi sent him on.

"Sheriff?" he said in the hallway, inching forward

past Mimi's bedroom, which had been totally over-
hauled. Gone were the girlish flounces and stuffed
animals. A man's decor warmed the room, with rich
paisleys and deep, elegant stripes. Jealousy fired at
the base of Mason's skull, but he strode on. "Sheriff?"

He definitely heard a moan, and it didn't sound like
one of pleasure. Taking a deep breath, he swung the
door open. Sheriff Cannady lay in bed, where he'd
obviously been all day.

"Sir?" Mason said, approaching the bed. "I'm
sorry for…" He stared down at the man's gray face,
eyes sunken with pain. Mimi would never have left
for Hawaii with her father in this shape. Something
had happened in the night. Fear swept over him. The
sheriff was ill, and he needed a hospital *now*.

"Hang on," he said, "I'm calling for help."

BY THE TIME the ambulance arrived, a group of Jefferson brothers were in the sheriff's hallway, waiting
anxiously. Bandera led the paramedics upstairs, and
then they all stood around helplessly watching as the
sheriff's vitals were taken. Mason shifted his hands
into his pockets. Matters weren't good, he could tell
that by reading the paramedics' faces.

He was going to have to call Mimi. His heart
turned over inside him. She'd said she really needed
this honeymoon with Brian. As much as that sent pain
through him, he'd heard the urgency in her voice. He

knew she would try hard to make her new marriage a happy one.

"I'm going with the sheriff," Last called from the stairwell as the sheriff was bundled off.

"I'll follow," Mason replied. "I guess I'd better call Mimi."

Tex turned to look at him. "What are you going to tell her?"

"That her father's gone to the hospital," he said on a heavy sigh.

"Maybe you should wait until you know more."

Mason nodded. "I'd rather put it off, that's for certain." He scratched his jawline. "You don't suppose he's in danger of…"

"No. Dying isn't in his plans. He's just real sick," Tex said. "What's wrong with him?"

"I don't exactly know. Mimi asked me to keep an eye on him. And I laughed it off because the sheriff's always been such a workhorse. I don't think he's ever had a day of sick leave in his life."

"I know what's wrong with him," Navarro said, meeting them on the stairwell as they went down after the ambulance driver had cleared away. "He's got liver disease."

"What does that mean?"

"It means he's got to have a new liver. Or else."

Mason stopped in his tracks and looked at his brothers as they gathered around. "Or else what?"

"He dies," Navarro said simply. "That's what the

paramedics got from the information on the sheriff's ID bracelet and a call in to the hospital.''

They stared at each other as the bright morning light showed worried faces, eyes full of pain. Overhead, a bird called. Mason could only register the sound and not the type of bird. His mind simply would not process. ''Die?'' he repeated. ''Sheriff Cannady?''

And that would explain Mimi's reluctance to take care of the Jefferson boys the way she always had. It was the reason for her quickfire marriage. It crystal-clear illuminated the urgency of her trip to Hawaii. If the sheriff was terminal—and from what Mason knew at this moment, the man's odds were slim—Mimi would want her father to see his only child married. Happy.

And most of all, she'd want her father to have a grandchild.

Mimi was trying to get pregnant.

''Mason?'' one of his brothers said, but he couldn't look up.

So fast. It was all happening too fast. She'd just gotten married. And yet, she was desperate, he realized. Maybe for the first time, she had not confided in him. Their relationship had shifted, and he was no longer the brother-in-fun he'd been. She'd tried to tell him, with her voice and her absence and her tense expression. He hadn't listened. He'd been too busy avoiding the marital noose with a girl who was, to his mind, his best friend. Everyone said they belonged together, but he hadn't wanted to see her that way.

He really could not see himself married. There was plenty for him to handle as it was. He had enough family, and Maverick's shadow was ever in his mind.

But now he wished he'd been just a little less protective of his heart. Because by protecting his, he'd forced Mimi to protect hers.

Chapter Ten

Ranger switched off the cell phone and looked at a very desirable Hannah. She was examining him like a hissing cat about to be loosed on his head.

"So, are they sending help?" she asked. "Maybe a guide to lead us out of here? A helicopter? My boat leaves tonight, you know."

"No, no help," he replied, trying to sound cheerful. "I vote we sleep on it."

She blew a raspberry.

"Everything will look better in the morning," he said, patting the bench seat. "And sleep is beneficial."

"Sleep together, no doubt."

"Of course, together. You said you wanted eight minutes." He gave her his best he-man grin, the one that melted all the women without fail. "I'm offering eight hours."

"It's not going to happen. You loused up your chance big-time. You know, it's no wonder you Jefferson boys have to break something to win women.

By the time you get through messing the whole thing up, you have to do something drastic.''

Her very tone told him she was not fooling around. Maybe he'd come on too strong with the caveman approach.

"You knew how much it meant to me to get on that boat, and you set fire to the map," she accused. "And you didn't ask Archer for directions out of here. I don't think you're trying."

"I don't know where we are, exactly. So I couldn't ask for help out of here. Plus, I didn't want to mention this before, but…we've got a flat."

"A flat!"

"And we may be a trifle low on gas. But those are minor issues," he assured her. "The big issue is simply that…we're lost." He hated admitting that, since he'd only planned to detour, an idea that had supremely backfired on him. "It will all work out, I promise. I'll get you to that boat and to your ex. Or almost-ex. Whatever he is," he said on a deep sigh.

"You're just saying that so I'll succumb, and it's not going to work. I mean, you nearly had me. But then you set the map on fire and folded papers burning brightly do not romance make." She crossed her arms and stared at him.

"No, I promise. I'm very good at recovery missions."

She snorted. "You rolled down a hill nude after impaling yourself on a poisonous plant. The only reason you recovered from that was because of Hawk."

He felt a tiny spark of jealousy, then forced it away. "Are we having our first fight?"

"Try multiplying that by ten. Because you and I both know I won't make it to the riverboat before it leaves. That's my employment, Ranger."

His lips compressed. What could he say? He'd had a pigheaded idea. "Sure are a lot of stars out to waste on bickering."

"You mean, gee, it's a great night, and we're stuck in the middle of nowhere with a flat, no spare, no compass and not enough gas to waste by driving aimlessly around on our rim, so we might as well play hide-the-salami." She gave him a stern eyeing. "Do I translate your machismo correctly?"

Whew-oo! This was a hot one! "Remind me of your saucy side if I ever ask you to marry me again. I may have missed that before."

"I don't want to get married. And I sure don't want to be with you, cowboy. Right at this moment, I'm so mad that I'm thinking perhaps I should have stuck with Jellyfish."

"What do they have to do with anything?" he demanded, annoyed at her illogical conversational turn—and the fact that she was right about everything she was saying.

"My ex. My friend, Jellyfish."

He stared at her, to see if she was telling the truth. Her eyes were clear and focused. He started laughing. He laughed until he felt better. Wiping his eyes, he said, "Wait till I tell my brothers that I've been jealous of a man named Jellyfish!'' And he threw back his head, roaring with more laughter.

Hannah flounced down in the seat and gazed out the window until he'd finished. ''I hope you didn't rupture anything.''

''Actually, I feel better.'' But now he didn't, because Hannah looked so dismayed. Damn, but he hadn't meant to hurt her feelings. It's just that he had been jealous, and clearly, there was no need. Jellyfish! No cowboy would ever have a name like that! He imagined an undersized, whitish, forty-year-old who was too sickly to do much more than steer a riverboat all day. Pursing his lips, he realized he had all the odds stacked in his favor, and he'd be the better man if he was big about his non-rival.

''I'm sorry, Hannah,'' he said. ''I shouldn't have laughed at your friend. And I shouldn't have picked on you. I'm feeling frustrated and embarrassed.''

Her lips separated as she turned to look at him. ''Well, cowboy, color me shocked. An apology?''

''Yes. And I also shouldn't have set the map on fire. I got carried away trying to…to get you carried away.''

She looked at him speculatively. ''You're kind of cute when you're not acting like an ass.''

''Is that the rude word with a French pronunciation you wanted to call me?''

''Sort of. Ah-shay,'' she enunciated, so he could get her inflection. ''Ah-shay.''

''Huh?'' He looked at her quizzically.

"The business orifice of the ass," she said with a comforting nod and a smile.

"Oh. I get it." He really didn't, but he wasn't going to let on. "Wouldn't that be ah-shole?"

"Oh, for heaven's sake." She rolled her eyes for his benefit, and then brightened. "So. You were jealous?" she asked, her eyes big and curious.

He started to fib, and then realized he'd already admitted it and was going to have to derail his ah-shay tendencies. "Still am."

"And your idea of romance was to start a little fire?"

"I lack resources in the middle of nowhere. And I heard women are seduced by fires."

"In a fireplace, you dip. I'm realizing that you may not be very good at this, for all your big talk," she told him. "If Hawk hadn't had all the necessary romantic supplies on hand, you probably wouldn't have known what to do."

"I found a brochure in the kitchen drawer that had tips for romance," he admitted. "That hideaway of Hawk's is a honeymooner's retreat he rents out."

"No way!"

"It's true."

She shook her head in amazement. "I can't believe you came clean with that admission."

"I'm trying to start this relationship out with honesty. I'm sort of a believer in that."

"Okay. You're not the smoothest man I've ever known. How's that for honesty?"

"Pretty good," he admitted grudgingly. "I'm used to women who do all the work for me. Lord only knows you don't help me out much."

"Pitiful."

He slipped her a sideways look. "Is it working?"

"Absolutely not. Now, if you had thought of roasting some vegetables on the map fire, I might have been impressed. I'm starving."

"That I can solve," he said, instantly cheered. Hopping out of the truck, he pulled some things out of a chest in the back. Getting back in, he handed her beef jerky and Twizzlers, then put cans of Big Red in the cup holders. "I travel prepared."

She gazed at his offering. "Well, it's not four-star restaurant fare, but I will not complain."

She tore into the beef jerky wrapper without any hint of a snit, he noticed with admiration. "I do like the fact that you travel well. You're not prissy."

"No, I'm not."

"Some girls would be really perturbed at the accommodations and sustenance—"

"My parents were hippies. We lived in a commune. I can adapt." She looked at him. "But I really, really want to know something."

He loved the way she was staring at him, her eyes round and big in the waning light. Green smells from the meadows blew through the truck on a playful breeze, and as he stared at Hannah, he thought he could stay with her like this for a long time. Maybe forever. She wasn't the most beautiful woman on the planet, she wasn't a cowgirl, and she wasn't settled, that was for certain. But something about her felt right to him.

It had to be the stuff Hawk had given him to drink. Maybe that foul medicine hadn't completely worked its way out of his system. "Ask. Whatever you want."

"You said you wanted us to have honesty between us."

"Yeah." He drank some soda and made a face. "Maybe I'll switch to beer."

"Pay attention," she told him. "This is an important question."

"I'm right with you, lady. Fire away."

"It was pretty hard for me to tell you I couldn't have kids," she said softly.

He stared at her. "Um, oh yeah. I forgot about that. I'm sorry you can't."

Her eyes grew wide. "You are?"

"Well, yeah. Isn't that what I should say?"

"I guess so."

But she put her jerky back in the package as if she'd lost her appetite. "What is it?" he asked. "I *am* sorry that you went through that."

Her gaze turned hopeful. "Nothing else?"

He scratched his head. "Hannah, you're going to have to ask me directly what it is you want to know. You've already determined my scale of logic and romance."

She swallowed and brushed her hands together before looking at him. "Does not being able to have a baby—"

"Oh!" he exclaimed. "No. That would not change my mind, if we were of a mind to be discussing a real marriage. No. I don't want kids. I haven't wanted marriage for just that reason. The family history and all that." He shook his head decisively. "No. Last's were the final diapers I ever hope to change, thank you."

She smiled at him. "And you don't mind a scar here or there?"

"A scar?" He realized where the conversation might be heading. His heart lit up. "Hannah, my scars outnumber yours any day, first of all. Secondly, I think I can say this for all men, we're much more interested in the destination than the um—" He broke off and rubbed his chin. "You know what? I'm going to insert my boot in my mouth when I should be saying something romantic."

She smiled and took his hand away from his chin. "Relax. I'm not looking for the perfect man. I'm not even looking for anything long-term, as you know." Moving his hand to her lips, she kissed his fingers. He was so startled that he picked up her other hand and did the same, only he kissed her fingers one at a time. Slowly. And then he kissed her lips softly, with pressure that communicated warmth, not heat. He wanted Hannah to know that there was more to him than raucous cowboy. He might not be skilled at verbal communication, but with his mouth he could tell her what he wanted her to know.

"I'll take that eight hours," she said. "There are too many stars out to waste on being angry."

His whole body exploded with desire. "I'll get you to that boat, even if I have to swim to it. I won't get you there by the time it leaves, but I will find it."

She nodded. "I know you will."

She trusted him, after all. That excited him more than anything. Leaning into her, he went for her lips, but she quickly stopped him with one finger. "We both agree that this is no-strings sex," she said.

"Agreed. This is casual coitus," he stated recklessly. Most women wanted to hear that a man loved them, but of course, Hannah would be different.

"Are you fibbing?" she asked.

"Yes," he said as he cupped her breasts in his hands. "Nothing about you is casual to me." He slid his fingers down her stomach, feeling the soft skin underneath her top. "Is that a problem?"

"Of course," she murmured. "Nothing about my upbringing is conducive to long-term stability. You're going to be disappointed by that eventually, and I don't want to be responsible for hurting you. Remember what your father said." She gazed up at him from under her lashes. "Maybe I'm not to your betterment."

He nodded slowly. "Maybe not." And then he unbuttoned her jeans. A slender thong encircled her hips with two small strings. His heart pounded. "Hannah, a certain part of my body wants you to know that you definitely are to my betterment,'' he said hoarsely.

He watched, mesmerized, as her hands went to her shirt, unbuttoning it to reveal a small bra. Polka dots brightened the material, shimmering in the moonlight. ''Happy bra,'' he said.

''Happy cowboy,'' she said, sliding the bra down her shoulders so that her nipples were bared.

''Oh, honey,'' he groaned. ''I've got to get in you. *Now*.''

She gasped as he pulled her bra off. ''Don't be too gentle with me.''

''Absolutely not.'' He removed the itty-bitty thong and made a slingshot out of it.

''I may never find that,'' she said, watching it fly.

He took her breasts in his mouth, and she tried not to sound like a delirious cheerleader when he sucked her nipples. ''Then again, all I care about is finding you.''

Her hands found the buttons on his jeans, and she frantically undid them. He took one second to help her pull off his jeans and everything else, and when she put her small hands on him, stroking and pulling, he wanted to holler yee-haw! But he used that energy instead to open the truck door, dragging her across the bench seat to him.

''Lie still,'' he told her, ''I've wanted to do this to you since I first met you.'' And he pulled her hips to his mouth, stroking inside her with his tongue until she cried out with a pleasure she'd never known before.

He sat her up and pulled her out of the truck onto him, and she locked her legs around his waist, and he thrust into her, and then she did scream to release the wild joy building inside her. He yelled, too, and she loved the sound of his pleasure, and the best part of this moment was that they were so far out in the middle of nowhere that nobody heard them.

BY THE TIME the sun broke night's hold on the darkness, Hannah was exhausted. She'd also had the best time she'd ever had, she acknowledged, pulling herself out of Ranger's arms. He was snoring in her ear, thoroughly satisfied, she thought smugly. They were lying on a blanket in the truckbed, and heaven only knew if she could jump down. His grip tightened on her when she tried to move away.

"Where're you going?" he asked without opening his eyes.

"To find my clothes, if that can be achieved." She removed his arms and crawled away from him, recognizing that she was probably going to be sore for a few days. Ranger had been good for his promise of eight hours.

He grabbed her ankle and gently dragged her back to him, which made her giggle in spite of herself.

"Not without my good-morning kiss," he told her bossily, flipping her onto her back so that he could kiss her thoroughly. "Now, that's how I like to greet the day,'' he said, when he was through ravishing her lips and most of her face and neck.

"I'm dying, Ranger,'' she said with a groan. "I've never had so much fun in my life. It was like riding all the fast rides at the amusement park all at once, over and over again.''

He stretched, revealing a big chest and strong muscles she hadn't had time to appreciate fully last night. Men weren't supposed to be so gorgeous. Nor so talented with their—

She'd pulled his shirt through the back window from where he'd tossed it, and a small rope circle fell to the truckbed. Picking it up, she held the ring up so that Ranger could see it. "What's this?''

He took the shirt and put it on, ignoring what she held up and the tone of her voice. "Your ring.''

"I know that. I threw it away in the cave.''

"And I picked it up.'' Jumping down from the truck, he went to shrug into the rest of his clothes. Was there anything more exciting than the sight of a man's bare butt hanging out below his shirt—

She forced herself to focus on her fear and not her attraction. "But why?''

He didn't look at her as he dressed. "Why not?''

Why not, indeed. This was supposed to be casual. It was supposed to mean nothing. He wasn't supposed to want anything serious between them.

Then why did he have her wedding ring?

"Ranger,'' she said, taking her clothes as he handed them over the side, "where is your ring?''

"In my wallet. Yours must have fallen out when I tore my clothes off. In fact, if we find all of your clothes, it will be a shock to me."

And then he looked at her with those big dark eyes, patient and kind and unmoving.

"You promised," she said softly. "You promised this was casual."

"I can be as casual as you want me to be." He leaned over the side to give her a soft kiss on the lips. "I'm going to go use the gents."

And he left her sitting there, naked in his truck.

She had the strangest feeling he had no intention of being casual at all. Suddenly, she was scared. If he loved her, if he was in love with her, she wouldn't know what to do.

She was afraid she might fall in love with him, too. She was nothing like the kind of woman he should love. Her way was to keep moving before anyone could realize she wasn't good enough. But a handsome man with a fairly stable lifestyle and enough badness in him to make cowboy sex the most fun she'd ever had—it was almost too irresistible.

He'd kept the wedding ring she'd flung in the dirt. Oh, God. She needed to keep moving. *Now.*

Chapter Eleven

"The ladies' is over by yonder tree," Ranger said cheerfully when he returned. "Hurry up. We've got to get a move on if we're going to catch that riverboat." And then he started singing.

The ass! He was actually serenading her with an old Mac Davis tune, one from, yes, her generation. It was the one about the girl getting that clinging-vine look in her eyes and the man warning her not to get hooked on him!

She jumped down from the truckbed without folding the blanket and ignored him, marching off to find the "ladies'" he'd offered. When she returned, he grinned at her.

"Feel better?" he asked.

She wanted to smack him. "It is so obvious what you're doing."

"Getting you to your riverboat, darlin'," he said too happily, gunning the truck engine. "Why, would you look at that? A full tank of gas!"

"What?" she exclaimed.

"Now, Miss HotKiss," he said, shaking a finger at her, his grin smug. "You didn't think a cowboy would travel in a truck this size without extra fuel, did you? Didn't you see that gas can back there? I believe you kicked it once or twice." He put his hat on and pulled out a good-size map from the console, which he made a great show of shaking out. "Now, I put us about here. Which means we're only five minutes from a main road. So we're off and running, huh, gal?"

He'd tricked her, the louse. Gritting her teeth, she said, "And the flat? Should I ask if meadow fairies fixed the flat in the night?"

"They did!" he exclaimed with wide eyes. "How did you guess? And you know what else," he said conspiratorially, "they even told me that the north star was a pretty reliable indicator of direction."

"You ass!" She crossed her arms and stared out the window.

"Some crazy little girl once upon a time told me the word was best used with a French pronunciation," he said, driving the truck up onto the highway smoothly, his grin even more smooth. "Ah-shay, I believe she told me. 'Course, by the time I finished with her, she was saying, Ah-Ranger!"

"Thanks for sharing that," Hannah said. "Very funny, I might add."

"Casual, sweetie," he said cheerfully. "I'm just a casual kind of guy, in case you hadn't noticed."

Whew! Hannah was pouting, which was good. Ranger's heart slowed down. She'd begun freaking out on him when she found her ring, and with her eyes all panicked and wild, she'd reminded him of a filly he'd once been stuck breaking in. That filly had just about worn him out with her crazy ways. Instantly, he'd realized Hannah was on her way out the gate.

But now she was calm—annoyed, but calm—and that was better. He'd need a few moments to gather his wits and prepare the rest of his battle plan. She was a wily one, never-tameable, and he'd have to be very careful about proceeding, sort of like stepping around grenades.

Obviously, she couldn't handle the thought of security or commitment. That was fine, wasn't it?

He tried to picture Hannah cooking on a stove, wearing an apron every day of her life, and the vision was enough to make him laugh. It was much easier to envision her naked.

He liked that image much better. Okay, so lots of sex could be in their future, just so long as she thought he didn't want her permanently.

Damn, that might suck after a while. Something inside him was stable, a part of him that overlaid his rowdy spirit. Did he want to settle down eventually? Not with the white picket fence, blue shutters and yard full of kids, but…settle with the right woman and wake up every day with a hard-on for her.

Beside him, Hannah was dozing. The sunlight

showed the softness of age in her face. He found that more attractive than any pretty young thing he might have had in his truck. So much about Hannah felt like what he'd been waiting for his whole life.

He could be patient, he told himself. He'd out-waited many a wild thing in his time.

He would take her to Jellyfish and his riverboat, and when she saw the two of them side-by-side, she would realize the difference between a squid and a cowboy. He would bet Little Miss Don't-Tie-Me-Down would jump into the river to swim after him as he waved goodbye!

A COUPLE OF SILENT HOURS later, they'd reached their destination. The riverboat shone white and serene in the murky water of the Mississippi.

"He's still here!" Hannah exclaimed, sitting up.

"Sure he is. I paid your almost-ex two hundred dollars per customer to hang around until we got here."

Hannah turned to stare at him. "What are you talking about?"

Ranger shrugged, pleased that he'd surprised her. "Last night, when you took a little snooze in between the action, I called Archer. I told him to make an offer to Jellyfish. That's what he negotiated on our behalf." He grinned.

"Our behalf?"

"I promised I'd get you to your riverboat, and here

you are. I always keep my promises." He winked
at her.

He had her unbalanced, Ranger thought with a
smirk. It felt good to unhinge her just a little. She was
impressed, although she didn't want to show it.

Cissy came running down the pier toward them.
"Hannah! You made it!"

Hannah jumped out of the truck, and the two
women embraced. Ranger beamed. Behind the
women, his brother walked down the pier toward
them, with another man beside him. Suddenly, Hannah separated herself from Cissy and went running
toward the stranger. She launched herself into his
arms, and he picked her up off the ground to swing
her around.

Which he could do easily, Ranger observed with
some dismay. The man was a brown giant. He topped
Ranger by a couple of inches and outweighed him by
a fit one hundred pounds. His arms, exposed by a
short-sleeved T-shirt, had hams for biceps. His face
was the youthful one of a twenty-something-year-old.
And he treated Hannah as gently as if she were a doll.
All the surety Ranger had felt began to shift inside
his chest.

"Ranger!" Hannah exclaimed. "Come meet Jellyfish!"

ONCE INSIDE the boat, Hannah put away her luggage
while Cissy looked on.

"Jellyfish was frantic when you didn't show up,"

Cissy said. "He was ready to send out the National Guard. Ranger's going to have to work to get on his good side."

"He's kind of protective of me." Hannah sat down on the bed and kicked off her shoes. "All I want is a shower."

"I'll leave you to it."

"Hang on a second, Cissy," Hannah said. "Ranger got me lost on purpose. I'm sorry it held up the trip."

Cissy shrugged. "I've made plenty in extra tips. I think I'm going to make more here than I did at Marvella's. And it's good, clean fun." She glanced around the room. "I think I could like living like this."

"Really? It suits the gypsy in me, but I would have thought you were looking for something more stable."

"I don't know." Cissy shook her head with a soft smile. "It's very romantic. I can't wait to get moving down the river."

"So, I guess Archer's pretty bored?"

"Who cares? He doesn't know what he wants any more than we do."

"Great. We're all just undecideds."

"Nothing decided between you and Ranger, then?" Cissy looked at her. "I know how much you like him, Hannah."

"I think I do. But…he's not a man one hauls around like luggage, and I'll never be the settled kind."

"Jellyfish told me the two of you grew up in the commune together."

"Yeah. We've known each other a long time." Hannah looked at her toes.

"Do you know he's talking about selling the riverboat?"

Hannah shook her head. "It won't matter to me."

"You won't marry him?"

"No. We talked about it, because we are so similar. He understands me. We come from the same place. But…that all changed when I fell in love."

Cissy nodded. "I can understand what you mean."

"And yet, I know Ranger wouldn't be the right man for me. In the long run, we wouldn't be happy together."

"So what are you going to do?"

Hannah picked up a brush and began working the tangles out of her hair. "I'm going to deal cards. That's what I came to do."

"And what about Ranger?"

Hannah put the brush down and leaned up against the wall, closing her eyes to enjoy the ever-so-slight rock of the boat. "Ranger can jump overboard for all I care."

"So do you think she slept with him?" Archer asked.

Ranger cursed. "I'm not going to think about that. In my mind, that's a branch of Hannah's extended tree that's going to get cut off."

"You realize you're basically in the position of being the twig," Archer pointed out. "How are you going to weather that? Did you see the size of him?"

"I've hung on bounty bulls. I've lived through Mason. I've endured Mimi's antics. Tell me one little girl's heart can't be stormed."

"I don't know, bro. Gentle Ben may give you some angina over Hannah."

Ranger frowned. "Did he talk about her?"

"Hell, yeah! I mean, do birds crap on windshields? He wanted to come after you, man. The only way I stopped him was telling him that she was in safe hands. I mean, he's like a wild man where Hannah's concerned. Apparently, she's the only thing that gets his blood up. Real protective is our Jellyfish."

Ranger scratched his head. "I can't say that she was exactly safe with me, man."

Archer's head jerked around like it was in a hurricane. "Shh! Dude! Don't even say that. Walls have ears and all that, and you, my twin, might get to walk the plank if the man even thinks you were mean to his baby."

"She is not his baby," Ranger said, as a spasm in his jaw clenched his teeth.

"He thinks she is. Hey," Archer said, staring at him closely, "you didn't make her cry, did you? I mean, what if she tells him? He's got thighs the size of your butt. Oh, man, I'm going to hate to see you get on the wrong side of him."

"Thanks for the support," Ranger said grimly.

"Listen, you're talking about a young man who grew up in a commune and looks like a pirate. The rules are different. Hell, we're not even on land!" Archer stared out the small window. "How far out to sea do we have to be before the laws of the land don't apply?"

"What are you talking about?" Ranger went to get a clean shirt from his duffel. "If he's got a beef, he can bring it to me. Otherwise, whatever happened between me and Hannah stays that way."

"You're in love with her, aren't you?"

Ranger hesitated. "I'm taking the fifth, for the moment."

"I gotta warn you, bro, you knew that she had issues. Those issues aren't going to go away just because you got her lost. If you didn't get the job done then, maybe it doesn't get done."

"Maybe Rome wasn't built in a day," Ranger snapped. "I'm sneaking up on her. And she's not the only one with issues."

Archer digested that. "True. Listen, Ranger. This little trip has taught me something about myself." He looked at his twin. "I'm not going any further with you."

"What are you going to do?"

"I think I'm going to Alaska."

Ranger didn't want to hear it. He knew what was coming. "Don't, man. He doesn't want to be found. At this point, I don't want him found. I don't need to see him."

"But I do, you know? I want to know what the deal is. Hell, life is short. Do you know I called home and Mason says the sheriff is real sick. He's like, bad. Like going down in a hurry."

"The sheriff?" Ranger's heart sank. "What happened?"

"Apparently Mimi was keeping a little secret under her hat. He's been sick for a while. Mason thinks that's why she got married."

"I don't get it."

Archer shrugged. "Her father's ill. She wanted him to see her happy. Guess that's why she got married on the fly. And now, if she can present the sheriff with a grandchild, don't think wild bulls won't keep Mimi from her destination."

"Hot damn."

"So, I've been thinking, bro. My e-mail relationship was about reaching out to someone with a kindred spirit. Anyone. But I don't want a woman yet. I'm not like you."

"I didn't want a woman, either, about a week ago," Ranger said grumpily. "In fact, I'm pretty damn sure I was a happy man."

"I know. And look at you now. You're a mess. And Jellyfish is gonna turn you into a pretzel if Hannah tells him you were less than a gentleman. See, I want to deal with my issues before some wily chiquita digs into my heart."

"Yeah, well." Ranger dug out a clean pair of jeans and threw them on the bed. "I have no desire to accompany you to Alaska. But I should. Actually, that's probably the best thing I could do.''

''There's always the military, too. You don't have to hang around here getting your heart broken.''

''Yeah. I see what you mean.'' There was a lot of truth that he hadn't wanted to see sinking into his thick skull. ''You know, after I broke that crazy filly the sheriff unloaded on us, she was never the same.''

''You asked for that horse, bro. In fact, you begged for her. Said only you could tame her.''

Ranger nodded. ''I remember only too well.'' But once broken, the filly had turned sad and passive. All that wildness wasn't just tamed; it was gone. It was as if she'd had to ignore the world to survive without her spirit. He'd always regretted it, and finally, he'd let the horse out to pasture for good, where she could get lost among the trees, a silver shadow he glimpsed every once in a while.

A knock on the door gave both of them pause. ''Yeah?'' Ranger called.

''Brother Ranger, it's Jellyfish. Got a second?''

''Brother Ranger?'' Ranger said to Archer. ''That sounded deceptively friendly.''

Archer looked at his twin. ''Try Big Brother Ranger. Whew! A second's all he's going to need with you. A second is all he'd need to take both of us out.''

Ranger sighed. ''He seemed peaceful enough.''

''Right. I'll cover you. But this is absolutely the last time I'm digging you out, man. It's getting too dangerous!''

Chapter Twelve

"Thanks, but I can handle it." Ranger opened the door and waved Archer out. "My brother was just leaving."

Archer and Jellyfish nodded at each other as Archer exited. Then Jellyfish looked at Ranger.

"Your offer for my lost time was generous. Was it a bribe?" Jellyfish asked.

Straight to the point. "If you're asking if I got lost on purpose with Hannah, yes, I did."

Jellyfish nodded. "You realize that if she'll ever agree to marry me, I'm going to be there for her."

Ranger nodded.

"She'll always be a part of my life."

"I figured as much." Not that he was happy about it, but there it was.

"What do you have to offer her?"

"I'm not sure yet. I'm trying to figure that out."

"Fair enough. But she's a sweet, smart, attractive woman. It would be best if you figured out why you deserve her. Very soon."

Ranger was starting to get steamed. Hannah had portrayed the relationship as one that had ended. Why was he getting the third degree? "Is there a problem I'm unaware of? Am I stepping on your toes?"

Jellyfish shook his head. "Just watching out for a special friend."

"Friend?"

"We grew up together in a commune. We understand each other. I know what her demons are, and I know what her angels are. And frankly, I don't need your money."

"I meant no insult by it."

"Just be sure you're serious about Hannah," Jellyfish told him. "You're welcome to come along, in fact, I invite you to do so. But no more getting lost. Hannah didn't look too happy when I asked her about you. That makes me very cautious, Brother Ranger."

He left the room, and Ranger sighed. "Great. This one's worse than Helga."

RANGER WANDERED into the gaming room that evening, his mind made up. Cissy looked glamorous in her hostessing outfit. Several diners obviously appreciated the scenery, and Cissy glowed with excitement. He wasn't worried about her safety, though; there was no doubt Jellyfish would take good care of the women on his boat.

Hannah was dealing cards, laughing with the players, mostly men, who could afford to lose chunks of change. Ranger admired her swift, small hands. He'd never seen her dressed as she was; she looked like a cross between an elegant woman and a sexy fairy. Whatever, she had the complete attention of her audience.

And, Ranger had to admit, she looked quite at home. He leaned up against a wall and contented himself with watching.

When it was time for a break, she came right over to him. "Thought you were going to gamble. Wasn't that why you decided to join me here?"

He nodded, playing along. "But I guess I'm not up for gambling tonight."

The smile left her eyes. "I think we should talk."

"Me, too."

She moved down a hall and took him into a chamber he swiftly realized was her bedroom. There were small decorations everywhere; beads hung from lampshades and the bedspread, while fringe hung from delicate curtains. It was eclectic and fun, and Ranger realized this was *her* room. Jellyfish kept this room just for Hannah.

"Now that we've left shore, things may change," she told him. "I'm going to be very busy. I'm afraid you'll get bored."

He recognized a blow-off when he heard one. She wouldn't meet his eyes, and her posture was stiff. He'd like to blame her withdrawal on Jellyfish, but he knew it had started after Ranger had made love to her, when she'd found that he'd kept her ring. He'd seen her panic. She looked unhappy now, and he couldn't bear that.

"It's all right," he said huskily, knowing that he had learned a lot from that silvery filly of his youth. "Archer and I talked. I've got some family duties I need to take care of."

She looked up at him.

"Mimi's father is ill, and she's out of town. She's getting home as quick as she can, but Mason's holding down an already-short fort. I need to get back. After that, I may meet up with Archer. He's going to take care of some other family stuff. I haven't totally given up on the military, but right now my services are needed back home."

"I see." Turning away, she kept her emotions hidden from him. "Well, I wish you the best of luck, Ranger."

"You, too." He put his hat on. "Well, I'll be getting off at the next stop. I need to take Hawk's truck back to his house, anyway. I'm going to let Archer drive mine on his jaunt."

She nodded. "Ranger, I haven't thanked you for bringing me here. It means a lot to me."

"I know. No thanks necessary. You saved my life. I'm glad I could do something for you."

"I did not save your life, Ranger. You would have gotten well on your own."

"Maybe." He nodded to her, hiding behind good manners. "If you ever need anything, call."

"I will."

He didn't figure she would, but he smiled and ruf-
fled her hair as he passed her to go through the door.

Casual.

HANNAH WATCHED Ranger leave, her emotions torn.
She was sad, but she was also relieved. A man like
him did not belong in her life; she could never make
him happy. As he'd said, he was needed at home.
Staying in one place would make her crazy. Shocked
that she'd fallen for the handsome cowboy, she'd decided to make an early return to the riverboat where
she usually worked six months of every year. Ranger
bringing her to Mississippi had been a surprise bonus,
but in the end, it hadn't made matters anything but
clearer.

They were not meant for each other.

Stepping out of the hall, she returned to the gaming
room. With a quick eye she scanned the boat. Cissy
was handling customers beautifully, almost as if there
was nothing on the planet she'd rather be doing. Jellyfish was chatting with regulars. Ranger was out of
sight.

She sighed. He was a home-man. He was steady.
He was strong and courageous and a little bit wild.
Real stubborn. Demanding. Opinionated. Focused on
her, if she wanted that.

She didn't want to be in love. She wanted casual,
something that didn't hurt. She'd known back in
Lonely Hearts Station that she'd fallen for this cow-

boy. It was clear then that her body had noticed him. It was clear now that her heart was hooked on him.

He would never be casual.

She missed him.

IN THE SMALL hallway a door opened, and a woman watched as Hannah went into the gaming room. Smiling to herself after hearing every word spoken by Ranger and Hannah, the woman closed the door again. Going to her briefcase, she pulled out a sheaf of papers and looked at them as if they were her best friends.

"Well, then. This will be easier than I thought it would be," she murmured to herself. "As soon as Mr. Jefferson leaves, we'll just have ourselves a *big* ol' breach of contract party," Marvella said. "Won't everybody who's invited be so surprised?"

And then she laughed as she settled down in the plush cabin to wait.

WHEN RANGER left the boat that evening, he had the strangest sense of foreboding. Since he wasn't normally a great one for prescient feelings, he decided he was suffering from post-Hannah syndrome.

She stood on the deck, waving goodbye to him, as did Jellyfish and Cissy. Archer got into Ranger's truck, and Ranger got into Hawk's truck, and they went their separate ways.

He didn't feel good about leaving Hannah, but it was the only thing he could do.

"WELL, NOW," Marvella said, coming up behind the bon voyage party. "Look what we have here. A real nice group of girls. And one big strong boy." She winked at Jellyfish. "Make that almost-man."

Cissy gasped, and Hannah watched her friend turn white and sag against Jellyfish. "What do *you* want?" Hannah demanded.

"I want my contract conditions honored," Marvella said smoothly.

"Who is this, Hannah?" Jellyfish asked.

"My name is Marvella. And this is my tracker who so easily helped me find you," she said, pointing to the Native American cowboy coming down the pier.

"Hawk!" Cissy and Hannah cried out.

"How could you?" Cissy asked. "How could you pretend to be my friend and then rat me out?"

Hawk didn't say anything. He looked at them, and then at Marvella, as if he weren't certain what was happening.

"When did she hire you?" Hannah asked. "Before or after you so magically healed Ranger?"

"That magic was from you," Hawk replied. "I was hired to track Cissy Kisserton. That's why I had you drop me off."

"So you could alert Marvella." Hannah shook with anger. "Why did you do this?"

"I track for anyone who needs help. Kidnap victims, missing family members. Runaway debts. I do not judge who is right or wrong."

"You didn't have to track us," Hannah pointed

out. "We were sitting ducks for you." She stared at Marvella. "So you found us. Big deal. Cissy's not going with you."

"Oh, I think she'll change her mind if the police have to get involved. Won't you, Cissy, dear?" Marvella purred. "Think about those youngsters of yours going without food. Think about your poor grandmother—"

"Stop!" Cissy shouted. Jellyfish put his arms around her to comfort her as she began to cry.

Marvella laughed.

Hannah stepped forward. "She owes you nothing. People lose employees all the time. You weren't a fit employer."

"Ah, well, that could be debated. However, she does owe me something." Marvella held up papers. "She owes me another year of service in exchange for her room, board and special payments to her family."

Hannah hesitated, stunned for a moment. Then she swung to face Cissy. "You didn't sign papers, did you?"

Cissy nodded miserably. "Yes."

Hannah looked at Jellyfish. He shrugged imperceptibly, telling her that it appeared that there was little they could do. Except, Hannah thought, push Marvella into the river. Maybe she'd melt like the wicked witch in the *Wizard of Oz*.

No. Marvella would float. She was so salty with evil that she would probably bob and laugh while

Hannah went to jail for battery. "You're a terrible person," she told Marvella.

"And you're sleeping with a cowboy for free." Marvella shrugged. "I don't do business that way, and guess what? I get to eat at night."

Hannah took a deep breath. "Take me instead," she told Marvella. "I'll work off her year."

"You?" Marvella laughed. "You, my dear, could never bring in the customers that Cissy does. Did you see the dining room back there? Men were hanging around because of her. They order extra drinks just to be around her. Tabs go up. Everything goes up, I might add. She's my golden girl." Her eyes roamed Hannah. "You're cute, but you're middle-aged. It's sort of…not the same."

"I'll buy out her contract," Jellyfish said. "Name your price."

Hannah flashed him a grateful glance.

"I thought you might offer, and I had a figure ready. But then I realized that money isn't everything," Marvella said. "Well, of course it is, but it's so much better when revenge comes with it." She snapped her fingers. "I'll cut her year in half if you come with her, Hannah."

"I don't get it," Hannah said.

"Oh, I think it'll be fun to watch Delilah suffer seeing you working for me." Marvella grinned. "I hope you give a decent haircut. And that your license is up to date."

Hannah blinked. Cissy was shivering. She looked sad and unhappy.

"I'm sorry, Hannah," Cissy said. "I should have told you I signed papers. I just didn't think Marvella would find me. I was hoping she couldn't get to me on the riverboat." She glared at Hawk, who looked embarrassed.

"Well, regret is never any fun," Marvella said sagely. "Do you want to come with me now, or should I get the local authorities involved?"

"That won't be necessary," Cissy said sadly, walking towards the pier.

Marvella pinned Hawk with a deadly stare. "And Mr. Tracker, don't you even think about getting any bright ideas about calling that cowboy on a cell phone. He'd better not hear from you that Cissy and wild woman are going to be so close to home."

Hawk walked away without replying.

THIRTY MINUTES LATER, Hawk grabbed the few things inside his cabin and headed down the hall. His job here was done—and for the first time, he didn't feel all that good about it. He never got into the morality and finger-pointing of cases. He tracked. He found. He signed off. Marvella had told him Cissy was a runaway relative who was in for an inheritance, and he'd detached himself from Cissy when he took the case, but now he wondered why his employer had lied.

An arm snaked around his neck, dragging him into a chamber off the hallway before he could regain his feet. "Shh, Brother Hawk," Jellyfish said in his ear. "You are in big trouble with me, dude."

Hawk estimated his chances of besting Jellyfish in a physical fight at about ten to one. He couldn't get off any good kicks in the small confines of the chamber, and the big man had the element of surprise. Hawk would just have to wait for an opening.

"I meant no harm," Hawk said. "I don't want to know anything about these people."

"Yeah, but see, they're not just people. Hannah is like my sister."

"Well, I didn't know Hannah would be involved. That I can swear to. Last time I saw Hannah, I left her with Ranger in a romantic cabin so they could work on their marriage."

"Marriage?"

The arm around his neck loosened slightly with surprise and Hawk seized his opportunity, slamming into Jellyfish's groin. The big man oofed, and Hawk grabbed the door, cracking it smartly into the riverboat owner's head.

"Better put ice on it," he told Jellyfish. "It's gonna swell."

And then he left the chamber, only to go sprawling on the floor. Hannah sat on his back, pulling his hair up so that she could see into his face.

"You did what you had to do," she said. "Now

I'm going to do what I have to do. Either you get hold of Ranger and tell him I need him like I've never needed anyone, or I'll send every grave robber, Native American artifact-hunter and junior newspaper reporter into your arroyo looking for the dinosaur bones and totems you're keeping to yourself. That *is* why you own that land, isn't it? To keep all that history to yourself?''

"There are no dinosaur bones down there," Hawk gasped.

"Maybe not," Hannah said through gritted teeth, releasing Hawk's head. "But you've done a wrong, and I know you want to fix this."

"I do not know about this being wrong," he said, gaining his feet and brushing off his clothes. "Those papers looked genuine to me."

"Yes, but Marvella is a bad person. She is mean to Cissy. Do you understand that?"

Hawk hesitated. "I don't want to hear this."

"No. You just want to be the hunter. You don't want to care about the prey. Well, let me tell you something, Mr. Tracker. This time, you've tracked a quarry whose heart is already fragile. She has a family that will suffer without her. Cissy can't be happy with Marvella, and it could kill her. Her spirit will die."

She had Hawk's full attention now. He nodded.

"You'll help me?"

He nodded again.

"Good. Remember what I said," she said, walking

into the chamber to help Jellyfish up. "Giant, pre-prehistoric, lizard-bird dino bones."

"Shh!" Hawk shouted, covering his ears. "I'll do my best!"

TOTALLY ANNOYED at the turn of events—and knowing he had to recover this mission since the old woman had lied to him—Hawk stopped behind some trees after he left the riverboat. He waited until a truck passed, and then he flagged down the next car. The driver was a gorgeous blonde, and she seemed real happy to have a cute Native-American in her car.

"You're sexy," she told him as he settled in next to her.

"You're not so bad yourself." He turned on the flattery. "I bet you think you saw me in a movie."

"No," she said goofily. "I think I saw you at the theater."

"I…see. I wonder if you by chance have a cell phone I can borrow?"

She giggled. "Of course. It's not safe to travel without one!"

It wasn't safe to pick up hitchhikers, either. "Thank you," Hawk said.

Swiftly, he dialed the local police. "I'm calling to report a missing vehicle. It's a truck. Yeah. Some cowboy fella took it heading due east. Not an hour ago, maybe. Hey, could you do me a favor?" He grinned at the blonde, who was all ears for the conversation she was privy to. "When you catch the guy, I don't want to press charges. I just want him to take the truck back where it belongs. Yeah. That's right. Okay, have him take it to the Never Lonely Cut-n-Gurls salon in Lonely Hearts Station, Texas. I know that's out of your jurisdiction, but if you tell him that message, I'm sure he won't require an escort. Thanks.''

Hanging up, he grinned. ''No one can claim that I called Ranger. Thank you,'' he said, giving the phone back to the blonde beside him. ''If you wouldn't mind dropping me off now, that would be excellent.''

''But there's nothing around here. It's not safe.''

He laughed. ''I'll be fine. Thanks for the ride.''

Chapter Thirteen

Ranger cursed when he saw the lights of the police cruiser behind him. "Just what I need." He pulled over and got out his driver's license.

A couple of state troopers came to his window, giving him an eyeing. Ranger eyed them back. "Is there a problem, officers?"

Officer Buzz-Cut nodded. "Stolen truck."

"Stolen truck! I didn't steal this thing. My truck beats this one hands-down any day. I don't have to steal a truck," Ranger stated.

"Owner called it in stolen."

"Hawk?" Ranger was stunned. "He loaned it to me. Why would he say I stole it?"

The office shrugged while the other one walked around the vehicle, checking it out. "We don't know. But he doesn't want to press charges."

"Well, isn't that fair of him," Ranger groused. "Could you tell him how very much I appreciate his thoughtfulness?"

"He wants you to take the truck back where it belongs."

"I was on my way." Ranger gestured toward the road. "I'm heading toward where the truck belongs. If I were stealing it, I would be going in the opposite direction, wouldn't I?"

"Just make sure you take it home, friend. Or we'll have to alert the authorities in Texas. I think it was very generous of the owner not to have you arrested, by the way."

"Oh, very generous." Ranger told himself to hold his temper in check, but it was hard not to take out his bad mood on the officer. Not that it would help, but many a Jefferson brother had lost his temper at an inappropriate time.

"Let's see." The officer pulled out a pad. "You're taking this vehicle to the Never Lonely Cut-n-Gurls salon." He gave Ranger a pointed look. "Is that right?"

Ranger's brows went up. "The Never—" Wait. Marvella's salon. Something was fishy. How would Hawk know about that place? Maybe Cissy had told him. But why would Hawk want his truck taken there? "I believe you are correct, sir," he said carefully.

"Is that where you're going or not?" the officer demanded testily.

"I'm on my way, gentlemen."

"Mind you get there. Otherwise the owner—"

"I know. Will have me rode out of town on a rail.

I'll just be getting on, officer,'' Ranger said, suddenly filled with an urgency he couldn't define. "Everything's going to be fine," he said, switching on the engine. "Thank you for stopping me!"

And he drove off, reminding himself not to exceed the speed limit.

But he felt that he needed to get to the Never Lonely Cut-n-Gurls salon *fast*.

So RANGER was sitting in Delilah's kitchen with her and Jerry, peering out the window, when he saw Marvella arrive in a taxi. "There's your sister," he said. Two women got out with her, and Ranger, Jerry and Delilah gasped. "Cissy and Hannah!" Ranger exclaimed.

And the only one of them who looked happy was Marvella. She was smiling like a cat, looking toward Delilah's shop, as if she knew she had an audience.

"What are you up to now, sister dear?" Delilah murmured.

"I'm damn well going to go ask." Ranger started toward the door, but Jerry grabbed him.

"Don't, son. I suspect you may need to retain the element of surprise."

Ranger hesitated. "Why?"

"Something's awry here." They watched the three ladies go inside the salon. Jerry pulled Delilah and Ranger away from the curtained window and they went back to their chairs. "You getting stopped and being told to go to Marvella's salon means someone was setting you up. Best you sit tight until we figure it all out. Marvella doesn't know you're here, I suspect, since I don't think she would have been the one to tell you to go to her salon. I think you'd be the last person she'd want to see.'' Jerry looked at Delilah. ''You'd know better than me, of course.''

''Not this time. Marvella is such a twisted sister.'' Delilah sighed. ''I don't think I should talk to her, either. Hannah is definitely her trump card, and that makes me more suspicious than anything. I agree with Jerry. We lay low for a while.''

AND RANGER had every intention of laying low. He'd left Hawk's truck out in front of Delilah's salon, knowing full well she would not be able to ID it.

But Hannah would remember the night they'd spent in it, together. If she knew he was in town, maybe she'd get in touch with him. Or maybe she wouldn't. Maybe she was with Marvella because she'd decided to work across the street.

But he'd bet his share of Malfunction Junction that wasn't the case. And he'd be here if she needed him.

HANNAH HAD NEVER SEEN anything quite like Marvella's salon. It was luxurious compared to Delilah's. The famous sparkly sign, proclaiming Save a Horse, Ride a Cowboy, was prominent in the main salon. The large hot tub was inviting, and candles glowed everywhere. Most salons smelled of hair chemicals.

Marvella's smelled of perfume and strangely enough, homebaked cookies.

The bedroom Marvella's receptionist, Valentine, showed Hannah to was inviting and clean. The decor was red, but softly done with white complements on the bedspread and drapes.

She could live here for six months, reluctantly. She was lucky her accommodations weren't worse. "Thank you," she said to Valentine.

"Whatever," Valentine said, flouncing out of the room and slamming the door behind her.

"*Whatever* is right," Hannah murmured. She hurried to the window and looked across the street at her old salon. Hawk's truck was still there—and that meant Ranger was, too.

In fact, there was a shadow upstairs in the window. A big one. Hope grew inside her, and she desperately wiggled the blinds to signal him.

Nothing moved across the street.

She glanced around the room for a phone. There wasn't one, so she returned to the window. The shadow was still there. Frantically, she moved the blinds.

Still, no reply. With a sigh, Hannah decided to go and shower. She could try again tomorrow.

A knock at the door startled her. Hurriedly, she closed the blinds. "Yes?"

Cissy came inside, closing the door behind her. "Can we talk?"

Hannah sat on the bed and motioned for Cissy to sit down, too. "Sure."

Her friend took a deep breath. "You didn't have to do what you did for me, Hannah." Cissy swallowed, her eyes tearing up. "I can't tell you how much I appreciate it. I don't think I could have borne a year with Marvella. I left because I couldn't bear another minute with her." The tears finally fell, unable to stop. "A year would have killed me."

Hannah put her arms around Cissy for a fast hug. "I know."

"You being here will make six months survivable."

Hannah pulled away and went to look out the window across the street. Hawk's truck was still parked there like a sentry. "We're not going to have to survive six months," she said confidently. "We're going to let a handsome prince rescue us from our ivory tower."

"What do you mean?" Cissy asked, reaching for a tissue to blow her nose.

"I don't know yet, exactly. The prince in this fairy tale-slash-rescue operation is an enigma." But a smile curved Hannah's lips. "Just don't unpack your bags yet, sister."

SOMETHING warm and strong and large crept into her bed that night, rousing her from a deep and peaceful sleep. Hannah started to scream, fearing that one of Marvella's customers might have found his way past the deadbolt on the door—until she realized only Ranger would be unfazed by a deadbolt.

"You ass!" she hissed. "Take your boots off before you get into bed!"

"Is that an invitation?" he asked with a chuckle.

"No." She reached to flip on the bedside lamp and caught her breath. For a prince, he certainly lived up to all expectations. Dark and handsome in jeans and a black shirt, he looked like the raffish, carry-me-away kind of bad man every woman dreams of. "Well, maybe."

Shaking her head, she commanded herself not to drool. "Did you see the blinds? What took you so long? And how did you get past the deadbolt?"

He pulled off his boots and leaned against the headboard with his hands behind his head, ever-so-casual, as his gaze roamed not so casually across her spaghetti-strap white nightie. "I saw your signal, and figured making after-hours calls was the accepted thing to do around here. I also didn't want to be seen, so now seemed like the best time to visit, and deadbolts are easy when one steals the key from Valentine's desk. Plus I wanted to know what you slept in when you're in an establishment of ill repute. I must say, you're not swinging with the scheme of things, baby."

She gasped and jerked the sheet up to her neck. "Could we just get on with the rescue?"

His expression was sardonic. "What rescue? I'm here to get a good night's sleep."

Her hand connected soundly with his thigh. "Pay attention, cowboy. You've got to figure out a way to spring me and Cissy from Marvella's clutches. Cissy's youngish. She was desperate. She shouldn't have to pay through the nose for a mistake anyone could make."

"Hmm. Interesting, I admit, but I'm only here to check up on you. Not to engage in another of your fantasies, although you do think up some doozies. Did I ever tell you how much I enjoyed your call-of-the-wild fantasy in the truck?"

He just about had her convinced that he wasn't here to do the prince thing because he certainly wasn't paying attention to the matter at hand. He could win prizes for denseness. "Ranger, why would you need to check up on me?"

"I need to find out why, when I last saw you, you were on a riverboat floating away. Now you've switched careers on me. See, I just can't figure you out, sweetie."

Hannah told herself that as soon as she was through with Ranger—and she *would* never lay eyes on him again after that—she was going in for a dental checkup to see how much enamel she'd ground off her molars. "I have not switched careers, Ranger. Marvella had Cissy sign an employment contract, which Cissy was running out on because Marvella will not allow her to break it," she said. "Now do you understand?"

"I think so," he said, and she wanted to slap him

for playing dense. ''I could probably think better if I was getting kissed, though.''

''Ha! I knew it! You are thoroughly despicable,'' she said, although the idea of kissing Ranger had definite appeal. ''If you were any kind of gentleman, you'd offer to rescue us, and then you'd wait and see what kind of reward you might receive.''

He rolled over, pinning her beneath him so that he could grin down into her face. ''Well, my little card shark, I wouldn't gamble on those odds. I believe you've already determined that I'm not a gentleman, exactly. As for a reward, I learned a long time ago that I take my payment up front. Wouldn't want anyone to welsh on me after all my hard work, you know. Some unscrupulous princessess might try to claim that I hadn't rescued them the way they thought I should have, or that I didn't hold my mouth right as I was sliding down the ladder with said princess in my arms, or—''

''I get the point,'' Hannah said acidly. ''You don't trust me.''

''In a manner of speaking, no.'' His gaze narrowed on her. ''Tell me a bedtime story.''

She sighed. ''Which one?''

''The one about you and Jellyfish.''

Uh-oh. She stared up at him. ''What do you want to know?''

''Is he old enough to captain a riverboat?''

She heard the annoyance in his tone and smiled.

"Now you see how it feels to be the eldest, Brother Ranger."

"Don't start that crap," he growled. "And where did he pick up such a stupid handle? I've never seen anyone look less like a jellyfish."

"No, he's pretty handsome, isn't he?"

"Hannah," Ranger said, his voice a warning as he pressed against her with something that felt very hard and wonderful between her legs.

She caught her breath. "We used to go to the seashore, the whole commune. He was the only one not bothered by jellyfish. In fact, he loved the way they lit up and sparkled. When red tide was in, the jellyfish would be scattered all along the shore in pieces, like beautiful, still-sparkling diamonds. The rest of us wore flip-flops, because the pieces could sting. But Jellyfish could walk all day along the shore and the stings didn't bother him."

"Big tough guy," Ranger said on a grunt. "What's he to you?"

"He's always been my protector," Hannah said, nudging her body up against Ranger's. "He was there for me when I couldn't count on my own family."

"He's not here now."

"No, but you are, and you aren't getting the job done," she said deliberately. "Still don't trust me?"

"I don't know. Probably not." And then he kissed her lips, soft and sweet, and then more hungrily, demanding that she give him reason to trust her.

She didn't trust herself right now, not with him on

top of her, with the bad intent in his eyes, and a major piece of something hot and hard jutting against her lower half. Oh, she remembered that part of him very well. In spite of all her good intentions to stay focused on the mission, she felt herself starting to heat.

She pulled away from his lips before she lost all her self-control and what little pride she had left. "You know, it would be just peachy if you'd get off of me, you big lug."

"Peachy?" Ranger repeated with a grin.

"That's the word," she said defiantly, trying to get her mind off what she suspected his mind was mulling by picking a squabble. "Do you have a problem with it?"

"Nope," he said, pulling the blanket out of her fingers and holding it tight so she couldn't jerk it back up. He winked at her. "Makes me think of your breasts." And he took hold of one of her spaghetti straps with his teeth and pulled that down, too, exposing her to his suddenly hot gaze. "Now these are peaches."

Hannah felt herself go weak. "Ranger," she said, feeling her resistance caving. "Could we focus on the task at hand? If we put our heads together, we can probably think of a way to outwit Marvella."

"You know, you're right," he said, tucking the stolen spaghetti strap under his finger with the blanket. "But then again, I believe we'd think even better if our bodies were together." And he took her nipple into his mouth, sucking it, biting it and tasting it.

"Oh, my goodness," Hannah said on a moan. "Yes, maybe you're right. I'm certain we think better together. Hurry, Ranger." She helped him strip off his clothes and giggled when he tossed her nightgown to the floor. And then he was on her, and in her, and his mouth was everywhere, and a scream built inside her that didn't seem to stop until she'd forgotten all about being rescued.

And when she awakened the next morning, her bed was empty and the door was locked. Her nightgown was still on the floor. She flew to the window and looked out.

Ranger's truck was gone.

Chapter Fourteen

Someone tapped on her bedroom door, so Hannah threw on her gown and robe and went to unlock it. Cissy walked in. "How's the latest escape planning?" Cissy asked.

"I'm going to kill that cowboy," Hannah said on a moan. "I thought everything was fine. But then he got away and now I think he was serious about not rescuing us." She took a deep breath. "Now we have to beam up Plan B."

"Wait. When was Ranger here?"

"All night, the cheater. He'd cheat a blind man at cards, I do believe."

"You're really miffed with him, aren't you?" Cissy observed wryly. "He gets your feathers out of place real good."

"It's just that I mean to say *no*," Hannah said, "but then I say yes, and then whatever plan I had goes the wrong way. I hate to say it, but that man really goofs me up." She sighed and checked the street again. No truck. "We've gone around in circles, you know. We left because we wanted a new life, but now we're back, and we still want a new life.''

Cissy nodded. ''I got a snake in my bed last night.''

''What?'' Hannah gaped at her friend.

''Well, it was just a garden snake. And the prank was so silly and so like Marvella's girls that it shouldn't have rattled me. But it did.'' Tears started to fall down Cissy's cheeks, and she wiped them away impatiently. ''They're not happy I'm back. Valentine told me that while I was gone, Marvella gave them more goodies. Lord knows *I'm* not happy to be back.'' She took a deep breath. ''I wish I hadn't signed that stupid employment contract.''

''How did someone get into your room?''

''I think the snake was probably put there when I went down the hall to brush my teeth. I left my bedroom door open.'' She shuddered. ''I really don't prefer snakes.''

''Where is it now?''

''I left it in the bed. The snake seemed real cozy, and I wasn't about to give any pranksters the satisfaction of a scream. I slept on the chaise lounge.''

''I'll get it. Show me.'' Hannah followed Cissy to her room, but the snake was gone.

''It's in here somewhere.'' Cissy's eyes were big. ''It's taken up residence in a drape or drawer or something!''

Hannah searched the room. ''If Ranger comes back, I'm going to tell him to hurry up with the plans.

Not that I think he's going to. I'm going to have to think up a way out of this myself.''

"You don't have to stay here for six months," Cissy said sadly.

"Yes, I do. Hang on. Here's the little devil." She removed the snake from the sheet it was content to curl up in. "Hmm." She held it up and looked at it. "Well, you'd be happiest in the garden, but if you don't mind, I think I'll have you do me a favor," she told the snake.

"Where are you going?" Cissy called as she left the room.

"To even the score." With the snake in her robe pocket, Hannah went down the hall. She heard voices outside one of the bedroom doors and stopped to listen.

"We've got to get her out of here."

"She won't go! And the snake didn't work. She didn't even scream, and she couldn't have missed it. I put it right in the center of the bed."

"We could pay someone to kidnap her."

"And then what?" someone asked snidely. "She'd just return once Marvella chased her down."

"Well, maybe we can find a way to make her less beautiful. How gorgeous do you think she'd be with short hair? Like, a half-inch long?"

Everyone giggled. Hannah rolled her eyes and opened the door. Three stylists jumped guiltily.

"Hello," Hannah said. "Oops, this isn't the powder room."

''Down the hall,'' one of the girls said. ''How long are you staying?''

Hannah's brows arched. ''Why, Miss Marvella offered to make me a partner in the salon,'' she said. ''And she told Cissy she was manager material.''

The gasps were silent and painful. They stared at her with dismay. Hannah moved closer. ''Oh, look at this pretty wedding ring quilt,'' she said. ''Did you make this, Valentine?'' All three women turned to stare at the quilt, and Hannah slipped the little snake down Valentine's silky robe.

The scream was instant and bloodcurdling. ''Get it out, get it out!'' Valentine shrieked, hopping around, shaking her robe. ''Oh, my gosh!'' And she exploded with another scream when the snake landed on her toes. ''Snake! Snake!'' She ran crying from the room, and one of the other stylists joined her, squealing with horror.

That left one woman staring at Hannah before her gaze dropped guiltily to the snake on the ground. ''It's just a small one,'' she said.

''Maybe,'' Hannah said, bending to scoop up the little fellow, ''but if it's something more unkind next time, I'll be angry.''

''Oh?'' The woman put her hands on her hips. ''And just what will you do about it?''

''Tell Marvella you're trying to scare off her best advertising. In fact, I think I will anyway—''

''Wait.'' The remaining stylist held up her hand. ''That won't be necessary.''

Hannah gave her a meaningful stare. "I'm glad we understand each other. And now, I want some information."

"I don't give out information."

Hannah held the snake up. "Snakey and I think you do, unless you want us to rat you out."

"I'll just say I didn't do it."

"And I'll say I heard you planning to cut off Cissy's hair, and I think Marvella will believe me because I'm what you'd call a hostile employee."

"A spy," the girl spat.

"Hey, I like that!" Hannah said cheerfully. "Hannah, the hair salon spy! Now listen," she commanded, "here's the part where you need all your focus. What does Marvella fear most?"

"I can't tell."

"But you know."

"We all know. Even you know, if you'd think about it hard enough."

"Delilah."

The woman nodded. "She hates her with a passion."

Hannah thought about that. "Delilah's not bothering her. Why doesn't Marvella just go away?"

"And leave all the money and handsome men to her sister? No, it's too much fun for Marvella to torture Delilah. She really enjoys it. And that's all I'm saying," the stylist said as she exited.

Hannah left, too, going to the back door to put the snake in the bushes outside. "Goodbye, small friend.

I'm sorry I used you as a scare tactic, but you did your part.'' The snake went off gladly, and Hannah went back inside the salon to her bedroom.

Ranger was sitting on her bed, his boots kicked off, eating doughnuts and watching TV. ''Where have you been?'' he demanded with his mouth full.

Her lips parted. ''You rat. I thought you deserted me.''

''I went to bring you breakfast in bed. Get back in and let me feed you.''

Hannah shook her head, still too unsettled by his disappearance to want to give in so easily. ''You can't hang around here, Ranger.''

He glanced around her room. ''I don't like you being here. It's seedy.''

''And snakey, too.''

''Well, there'll be none of that, I can tell you,'' he said definitely. ''The only snake you're having is—''

''Ranger, please.'' Hannah didn't want to think about sex. She didn't have time to get sidetracked. ''Can you help me think?''

He waved for her to lock the door and join him on the bed, which she did, adopting his pose and taking the doughnut he handed her. They both stared at the TV, which was running endless commercials.

''I don't know if I can help you think, but my stomach's fuller, so we can give it a shot,'' Ranger said.

''I need Marvella's weak spot. Something I can bribe her with so that she'll let Cissy go.''

Ranger frowned. ''Bribery's kind of seedy.''

Hannah blinked. "Ranger, it *is* seedy. When in Rome, you live like the Romans do."

"I heard that. But I never believed it. I always live like a Jefferson cowboy. And I don't do blackmail."

She looked at him. "Okay. So how do I extricate Cissy and myself from this mess?"

"Well, first thing, you hire a lawyer. Of course, that's just my suggestion. You don't have to act on it—"

"A lawyer?" Hannah echoed. "I don't know a lawyer."

"I do. I already called him. Mimi's husband, Brian."

Her jaw dropped. "You already called him?"

"Mmm. He said to bring him the contract so he could review it. Brian says he's not yet seen a contract so airtight he couldn't find a loophole. Or a payoff, but we won't discuss that. To get you out of here, I'll be willing to chip in. Something. A buck or two."

Hannah threw her arms around his neck. "I knew you couldn't be as heartless as you were acting! All that baloney about not rescuing me! Ranger, you're such a sweetie!"

He allowed her to kiss his cheek and his ear and his cheek again, and then he pulled away to lean back against the headboard. "There's two problems we have to work through. One, we need a copy of the contract, which I don't think Marvella is going to give us. Unless Cissy kept a copy, and a nagging suspicion tells me she didn't."

"So we'll borrow it," Hannah said. "I don't mind borrowing for a good cause. This is definitely a good cause."

"Yes, but stealing's seedy," Ranger said.

"Excuse me," Hannah said, putting out a hand to stop him from inserting another doughnut hole into his mouth. "When did you become so righteous and…and…righteous? Are you not the man who deserted his family to join the military? Or at least go on a time-out with the illusion of going into the military?"

Ranger grunted. "The second problem I see is larger. It involves the charity rodeos and all that goes with them. It involves Delilah, even. Now, if we think this through," he pontificated, "we can see that Marvella is no purist when it comes to getting her way. Absolutely nothing comes between her and a dollar sign. And if we have a legal beagle look at her contract and deem it bogus, then she's going to be annoyed. Annoyance is not good for Marvella, because she's going to visit that on someone. In this case, I'm figuring that the unhappy target is Delilah."

"I'm following you, but at a remote distance," Hannah said, confused. "Marvella's always taking everything out on Delilah."

"Yeah, but springing Cissy with the help of a lawyer would really make Marvella mad. And we've got a good thing going between the two salons with the charity competitions, which may be benefiting Delilah more than Marvella right now, because Delilah's picking up new customers. Nobody from out of town knows the two salons hate each other, so Lonely Hearts Station gains economically. But say we piss off Marvella and she decides not to have anything to do with the rodeo, just to spite Delilah. Then we've hurt everybody on our side of the street.''

"I think I see." Hannah admired Ranger's ability to think through a sticky situation. "So what are you suggesting?"

"Well, Marvella's looking for money, right? That's the purpose of her hunting Cissy down.''

"No, that was just plain meanness.''

Ranger nodded. "Granted. But what if we throw her a huge bone, and slip Cissy out from underneath her paw while she doesn't realize what we're doing?"

Hannah sighed and got up, stretching.

"Could you do that again?" Ranger asked. "Stand in front of the window where the light shines through, please.''

She gave him a dry look. "Just go on with your nefarious thoughts. Not seedy, not dishonest. Just intricate and nefarious.''

"I say we offer her a deal. Something big. Something that involves money and cowboys, because that's two things I see she has ultimate respect for. Something that she can't say no to. A deal-maker and deal-breaker at the same time. Think, Hannah, think. It's gotta be novel. It's gotta be enough to smoke her out and make her say yes.''

"Um, um, um—" Hannah said, squinching her

eyes shut to concentrate. "Money and cowboys. What woman doesn't love money and cowboys?"

Ranger tapped her wrist. Her eyes flew open to see him in her face, staring at her intently. "Are you thinking hard? Or are you stuck on money and cowboys? I might be a bit jealous if you can't get past the cowboys part."

"A bachelor auction!" Hannah exclaimed. "At the next rodeo, we'll hold a bachelor auction for all your brothers and let Marvella have the proceeds in exchange for terminating Cissy's contract!"

"Uh-uh," Ranger said. "Absolutely not. My brothers would kill me! And besides, if it's just money Marvella's after, we can take up a collection and buy her out."

"But cowboys," Hannah reminded him. "You said we needed cowboys. And my idea has lots of cowboys."

"Yeah, but…" He was going to say that his brothers wouldn't work in such a scheme—they were no beefcakes. But then he realized what a stupid thought that was—they *were* beefcakes. They loved being drooled over and fought over and fighting themselves. It was just the type of harebrained—Ranger silently pardoned his play on words—shindig that they'd sink their teeth into. Tex in particular might have an itch to get involved in any rescue operation where Cissy was the prize.

"Well, maybe," he muttered. "It's a pretty stupid

idea, Hannah. In fact, it's so…seedy that it just might work.''

''Wait till I tell Cissy! Thank you, Ranger. It's a brilliant idea you thought up! Everybody wins!'' She kissed his cheek and went running out the door.

Ranger leaned his head back against the headboard with a thump. ''Oh, no,'' he said. ''Not a bachelor auction. Why didn't I see that one coming?''

BUT WHEN Marvella got wind of their proposition, she turned it down flat.

''Absolutely not,'' she said. ''I'm enjoying having Cissy here, and Hannah as my guest. And no amount of money can pay for enjoyment of that kind.''

Marvella grinned at Ranger, who was sitting on Hannah's bed as he had been doing off and on for the past two days. Her eyes lit with greedy amusement. ''And Mr. Jefferson, as far as I can see, you have not been granted exclusive visiting privileges for this young lady.''

Hannah gazed at Marvella in dismay. She couldn't commit to keeping her hair one color. Exclusive privileges?

''You can't keep coming here, Mr. Jefferson. I'm certain you'll understand that this establishment has standards. Why should I allow one customer not to pay?''

Ranger narrowed his eyes. ''I don't like what I think you're saying.''

''Well, let me put it to you this way. If other customers see that you have what we call run-of-the-house, they're going to assume that they can, too. After all, they are paying clients. You are not. And, as you can see, gentlemen do not freely roam our halls. It's not good for the girls' reputations or their safety.''

''Well, Ms. Marvella,'' Ranger said, his patience shot and gone, ''I hate to break this to you. I really was holding back on this because it's important to Hannah to be loyal to Cissy. But this woman,'' he said, putting his arm around Hannah, ''is my wife. And I'll see her when I damn well please.''

''Well, in that case,'' Marvella said, her nostrils flaring with anger, ''we have a problem.''

Hannah shrank away from the fury in Marvella's eyes. She'd seen many emotions on Marvella's face, but this was the most frightening one.

''You will leave at once,'' she told Hannah. ''You and your cowboy husband. And Cissy's contract reverts to the original terms. One *full* year of employment.''

Chapter Fifteen

"I'm sorry," Ranger told Hannah as she tossed her leopard-printed luggage into the back of Hawk's truck. "I shouldn't have said it."

"No, you shouldn't have." She glared at Ranger across the truckbed. "You're so possessive, Ranger, and it's the one thing that will not work with me. And you know it. I am not your wife. I will not be your wife. I only married you to give you a reason to exit your phobic state. We don't even know that Hawk marrying us was legal."

"We don't know that it wasn't."

"Well, I didn't sign any papers. And it wasn't orthodox. As far as I'm concerned, it didn't happen. If you need further convincing, have Brian draw up divorce papers. And burn those stupid rings. Right now, I'm going inside to call Jellyfish and find out where the boat is, and then you're going to take me there and leave me there and never see me again. Understood?"

He'd really blown it. If there was one way to chase

Hannah off, it was to act like a big, fat, chauvinist pig. That's what he'd been, and now he was getting slaughtered. Which he richly deserved. "What about Cissy?"

"I did my best," Hannah said. "Thanks to you, I'll have to get out of town and think for a while and see what else I can come up with. Now, I'm going to call Jellyfish."

She walked away, and Ranger sighed. "Stupid. Stupid." He smacked his head and said it again. Everything Hannah said was right. And the tears in Cissy's eyes when she realized her contract had reverted to its original terms was more than he could bear.

Bottom line: Hannah had helped him with his phobia, the Curse of the Broken Body Parts. He had not helped her with her fear of commitment. In fact, he'd done the very worst thing possible.

But he couldn't take Hannah to the riverboat. Once she said goodbye this time, it would be forever. His heart couldn't take it.

Quietly, he laid Hawk's keys on the seat for her to find. And then he left.

DELILAH HUGGED Hannah when she went into the Lonely Hearts Salon on the pretext of needing to use the phone. The other stylists gathered round, and the pet chicken squawked from her place on a shelf.

It felt as if she'd come home. With tears in her eyes, Hannah told them everything that had happened.

"I can't think of a way to spring Cissy," Delilah said. "You gave it your best shot. She did sign a contract. She does have this obligation. There's not much else you can do, honey. You can't save the world.

"But you might not want to be so hard on Ranger," she continued. "After all, Marvella's the kind of woman who makes people say things they normally wouldn't. And do things, too."

"I know." Ranger had been trying to help, not hurt. But he'd still scared her. "It's something I have to work out," she told Delilah. "I start to shake when I think about being connected to one person for the rest of my life. And Ranger's the kind of man who shakes when he thinks about something of his getting stolen, or lost, or taken away." She shook her head. "I'd make him crazy, Delilah. He wouldn't be happy with me."

"Take some time to think about it. I'll keep an eye on Cissy."

"Thanks." They hugged goodbye, and Hannah squeezed the older woman tightly. It felt so right to be saying goodbye the way she should have done the first time, instead of protecting her emotions by running out. She let the sensations of sadness, and sentiment, and happiness wash over her. She would miss Delilah. She would miss the women of the Lonely Hearts Salon. They had changed her for the better.

She hugged each of them in turn, feeling the mist

of tears in her eyes. It was hard to let herself feel the pain of separation, but it also felt like she'd finally made it to the other side.

"Oh, THAT'S just great," Hannah said when she saw the keys in the seat and realized Ranger had gone AWOL. She got in the truck, started it up, and with a last glance at Marvella's enemy camp, she drove away. It hurt to leave Cissy behind, and her mind dealt and re-shuffled ways to free her from Marvella.

If she'd sneezed, she would have missed the lone cowboy loping toward the gas station at the edge of town. She stopped the truck for a moment.

"Two options," she muttered to herself. "One, I run you down, you big chicken. Anger dispersement. Two, I pass on by and act like I didn't see you. Anger displacement. Heaven knows you weren't of a mind to stop when you first pulled through Lonely Hearts Station, and if it hadn't been for Cissy stopping you, I'd still be hitching."

On the other hand, look how much fun they'd had on their road trip. And he had gotten her to the riverboat as promised.

Maybe it was best not to part on unhappy terms, as Delilah had hinted.

"And then there's anger overcoming," she said with a sigh, pulling up beside him. He turned to look at her, his face wary. She put the window down and gave an arrogant sniff. "I hear you drive better than you talk, cowboy."

"That may be true," Ranger replied, his gaze cool. "But I'm not going to drive today."

"And a little birdie told me you make love in a truck seat the way a woman likes."

He shrugged. "That also may be true. But I'm not making love today."

They stared at each other. Hannah's heart started beating harder. "I've got no particular place I need to be."

His gaze cooled further so that his eyes looked like black ice. "I'm going home to the ranch. Where I belong."

That was a direct hit. His tone told her how much he hurt. "Want a ride in this shiny truck?"

"Not particularly. I'm going in here to call one of my brothers to come get me."

Hannah lowered her gaze for a second. "Ranger, I'd like to take you to Malfunction Junction."

He shook his head. "It's not necessary. Hannah, we had a lot of fun, but that's all you're looking for. And frankly, that's all I should be looking for. I got carried away, I admit it. And I'm sorry. But you know what?" He looked away for a moment, then returned to her gaze. "I'll catch you on the flip side."

And then he tipped his hat and went inside the gas station.

She closed her eyes, shaking her head. "Drive on by. Run him over. Those are my only two options left. Eenie, meenie—"

The driver's-side door jerked open, and Hannah

screamed. "Zowie!" she gasped. "Ranger, do you have to be so unpredictable?"

"Yes," he said. "Apparently it's self-defense. Please scoot over 'cause if we're going anywhere I'm driving."

"I—"

He narrowed his eyes on her.

"Okay. You know the way to Malfunction Junction better than I do."

"Actually, I just feel safer with me behind the wheel than you. Now, let's say as little as possible, and then you can drop me off and head on your airy-merry way."

"That's all well and good for you, but Malfunction Junction is in the opposite direction to the riverboat. Just a small thing I thought I'd point out. It's not like I'm dropping you off. I'm going about four hours out of my way."

"Yes, we are." He turned on a country-and-western station, loud enough to make conversation uncomfortable.

She switched off the radio. "We could be mature about this."

"We could," Ranger agreed, "but it probably wouldn't feel right."

Pursing her lips, she said, "Fine. Wake me when we're there, Hard Case."

RANGER GRUNTED when Hannah fell asleep beside him. She looked so cute and trusting when she was unconscious! But that was the problem. She wasn't cute and trusting. She was insecure and unwilling to change.

And he had clobbered her attempt to rescue Cissy, which had done nothing for his hero status. And as she'd pointed out, he didn't exactly trust her, either.

So they were both retrenched in their former positions. "It's a bad sign," he murmured. "A relationship should be easier than this. I was afraid of broken body parts, but I think a broken friendship might be worse."

One could be recovered from. One couldn't.

This one didn't feel like it could be recovered. They were uncomfortable with each other, and were basically together right now out of necessity.

That didn't feel very good. Of course, they'd started on the first road trip out of necessity.

But now he'd let her down with Cissy. What really stunk was not being a hero when your squeeze wanted you to be.

"Hey," he said, tapping Hannah on the thigh. "I know you're not really sleeping over there. You're just trying to get away from me."

"And it was working, too."

"Have you realized the only time we didn't get upset with each other was when we were having sex?"

She settled her gaze on him. "You can only do the truck thing once, Ranger."

"I'm not proposing we wear out Hawk's truck,"

he said. "I'm only saying that's a bit odd. We get along on one level, that's something to start with."

She wrinkled her nose, which he thought was adorable, in spite of himself. "I don't need a boy toy, thank you, though."

"Well, every woman needs a boy toy," Ranger rejoined. "I know I need a girl toy."

"Buy a Barbie," Hannah suggested. "She won't open her mouth, and she won't have commitment issues. She'll like sitting on your bed waiting for you to get home. In fact, she won't care either way."

He rubbed his chin. "Hannah, you're angry with me, and I understand that. I really do. But I think you're upset that I didn't live up to your ideal more than that I didn't rescue Cissy."

Her gaze narrowed. "What are you talking about now, Ranger?"

"That it may be a pattern with you. You look for a rescue. If someone doesn't live up to your expectations, you're let down, although all the while you were claiming what a free, independent lass you were. If you really were so uncommitable, you wouldn't look for a rescue in the first place." He glanced at her. "You throw people away, Hannah."

She blinked.

"Well, you said Jellyfish always rescued you. But he plays homing roost for you so that every once in a while you can fly back to safety. And then Delilah took you in. And then I tried to take you in, except I upset you because I wanted a bit more than you could give. But you led me on, let me think there was a chance, so that I'd rescue Cissy—and you. Now you're all disappointed because I didn't save the two of you the way you wanted me to, so you're moving me to the side.''

''Well, not totally,'' Hannah pointed out. ''I'm giving you a ride home, which is not exactly a lovely experience, considering you're playing Ranger Jefferson, nonprofit psychologist, all the way to Malfunction Junction. So *I* rescued *you*. And I'm annoyed because you told Marvella that cockamamy story about us being married. Which we are not.

''The truth is, Ranger, you didn't want me there, and you knew Marvella would have no use for me if I was married, and so you spilled the beans. See,'' she said, taking a deep breath as she got wound up, ''I see the situation a bit differently than you do. I see a stubborn chauvinist who has to have everything his way.

''It's a man's nature to be very simple in this regard. He sees woman, he wants woman, he takes woman by any means necessary. You're miffed because you didn't have the goods to get Cissy out of her mess, because it would have made you look like a hero to me. I don't think a man who lives in a place called Malfunction Junction should hang out his therapist's shingle just yet,'' she finished.

''Whew-ee,'' Ranger said. ''You said all that with only one breath. You are such a hotheaded little thing.''

She held up a hand. "Don't start."

"Well, I'd say you obviously have me firmly checkmated," Ranger said cheerfully.

Her glare held suspicion.

He grinned.

She closed her eyes and told herself to go back to sleep. But, in spite of her heated words, she knew Ranger had a point. Not that she was going to admit a thing.

"You're such an ape," she murmured sleepily. "You might evolve sometime in the next thousand years."

"WAKE UP, sleepyhead." At the ranch, Ranger stopped the truck, then he got out and left Hannah to stare after him, with the keys in the ignition like a pointed hint. And she *would* have driven off, but she had to use the ladies' accommodations.

Ranger could jolly well quit acting as though he was holding some awesome hand. She wasn't going to sit in the truck until he developed manners, her bladder wouldn't hold out long enough.

"Oh, Ranger!" she called, leaning out the window and pressing on the horn. "Help! Help!" she cried in a loud falsetto.

Several cowboys came out on the porch to stare at the commotion. Ranger hesitated, then turned around to glare her way. She waved urgently. Ranger was giving in, she could tell. The decibels she generated unnerved nearby cattle at the least. She honked again, and he came toward the truck at a jog.

"Hannah! The sheriff might be trying to sleep!" he told her.

"The sheriff?"

"Yes! He just got home from the hospital. Mimi and Brian had to return from their honeymoon in Hawaii so she could nurse him. And I realize they're way over there, but you sure were stirring up a ruckus." He glanced toward his brothers, though, and she knew he was more worried about them than the sheriff.

"You were being rude," she told him. "I have to use the powder room."

"Yes, I was being rude, and I shouldn't have. I was trying to teach you a lesson. Come on."

She let him help her out of the truck and followed along. "What was the lesson? How Not to Win Friends and Influence People?"

He groaned. "Never mind. The lesson plan was no good."

"Hi, guys," she said to Ranger's brothers as he dragged her past them.

"Hi, Hannah," they all said.

"Now, please make yourself at home, which I know you will," Ranger said. "The bathroom is upstairs."

"Much better!" Hannah said. "You know, you're not really an ogre, when you try."

"Fine, fine," Ranger said. "Well, get on with it. Up the stairs. Trot, trot."

It was too much fun annoying him like this. Hannah couldn't resist an impish smile as she went by. "Are we still angry with each other?"

"I think that would be a waste of time," Ranger said.

She smiled and walked up the stairs.

"But the view is nice," Ranger called after her. "I admit it, from where I'm standing, life is very pear-shaped."

It was a sweet compliment. She turned to look at him.

"For an older woman, you're well put together," he teased. But she'd heard the heat under his previous compliment.

They stared at each other.

"Ranger," Hannah said, but when she walked toward him her foot slid on the stair Helga had just finished polishing. Gasping, she clutched for the rail. Ranger instantly tried to catch her, but he was at the bottom of the staircase and she had several steps to tumble down before she reached him.

His brothers rushed in when they heard Hannah scream.

"What happened?" Last demanded.

"Hannah, are you all right?" Ranger asked, holding her in his arms.

She moaned, thinking Ranger's arms were a great,

safe place to be. There was a stinging twist to her ankle.

"It's your boneheaded Curse of the Broken Body Parts," Tex pointed out. "Only you visited it on Hannah!"

All the brothers groaned. Hannah hid her face against Ranger's chest. Maybe she should give him one more chance to rescue her; maybe she should give herself one more chance to get it right. "My ankle," she said on a small dramatic moan.

"Oh, no," Ranger said. "When I married you, I must have put the curse on you. I am so sorry, Hannah."

"Married her?" Mason said, catching an earful of that.

"A medicine man married us to get me over my fear of commitment, only Hannah's fear is bigger, so my curse obviously hit her," Ranger explained.

"Okay," Mason said. "I've heard enough nonsense. Carry Hannah upstairs and put her on the bed. And then call the doc. I don't know the first thing about women's swelling ankles. Helga, ice, please. And then, Ranger, I want to know why you decided not to inform your family about your wedding, much less invite them to it."

He glared at his sibling. "This may be a sinking ship, it may even be a bit wild. But one thing we, by crackey, will do is honor the state of matrimony.

"Bandera, call Brian and inquire as to the legality

of marriage ceremonies performed by medicine men. If it's legal, fine. If it's not, someone call the priest. Have him exorcise this stupid curse out of Ranger's brain!''

Chapter Sixteen

In the privacy of a guest room, Mimi looked at Hannah's ankle. "It doesn't look very swollen," Mimi said. "I think you were lucky."

"I'm probably faking it just a little," Hannah admitted. "I mean, it does hurt, but not so bad that I can't drive out of here. I might be looking for an excuse to stay."

"Oh, I see." Mimi nodded her understanding.

"I'm sorry about your father. I wish I could do something, Mimi."

Mimi nodded again. "So do I. But thank you."

Hannah looked down at her fingers for a moment. "I haven't talked to my folks in about a year."

"Really?"

Hannah nodded. "I never think about them being sick. I just don't think about them at all."

"Well," Mimi said. "I feel that way about my mother."

"You do?"

"Yeah." Mimi sighed. "She's out there somewhere, doing anything but being a mother. So I don't think about her.''

"Ranger says that I expect people to rescue me, and then if they don't, I sort of discount them.''

"That comes from being let down. I know that I've resolved to be a better mother than mine was.''

Hannah's eyes widened. "Are you…expecting?''

Mimi was quiet as she looked out the window for a moment. Then she turned to Hannah. "If there's been a miracle, yes. I certainly hope so. But Hannah, if you don't mind, don't share that with Ranger, or anyone. The Jefferson boys are not the only ones who have superstitions.'' She sighed deeply, and the sound was tired and sad. "I'm too afraid to believe in miracles anymore.''

WHEN RANGER came in to check on her, Hannah had been doing a lot of thinking. "Hi," she said.

"Hi. How's the ankle?''

"Fine. It's good enough for me to drive now.''

He glanced toward the window. "It's late. You should probably spend the night.''

"Will I be an imposition?''

He looked at her. "Aren't you always?'' But his tone wasn't mean.

"What do you mean?''

"I thought that was your goal. You impose yourself on people and then when they get used to you, you disappear, taking part of their heart with you.

Only by then, you're long gone and calling it just friends."

"Ranger, you don't sound coherent."

"I heard you tell Mimi that you were faking your ankle sprain."

Hannah's gaze slid away. "You claimed I wasn't impressed with how you rescued me. I thought I should give you a second chance, and find out if you were right."

"Yes, but this time I'm not going to rescue you, Hannah. So you're wasting our time."

"Ranger—"

He shook his head. "If I stay in here another minute, I'm going to dive into that bed and make love to you, you little faker. But then you'll just run off again. And I think somewhere under the curse and the arguing and the fake marriage, I was hoping you would fall for me the way I was afraid I was falling for you. Only, you *can't* fall for me, because you've got a built-in safety valve."

"I'm trying, Ranger," she said. "I'm here, aren't I?"

"Faking it." He shook his head. "The really bad news is that Brian made some phone calls. Guess what? Not only is Hawk a true medicine man by the standards of his tribe, he is a legal, ordained minister."

Hannah gasped. "Oh, God. I attacked a man of the cloth! I'm going to hell for that, don't you think?

Wouldn't you think that gets me a first-class ticket on the H-train?''

Ranger stared. ''Uh—''

''I don't get it,'' she said. ''So, he marries people and then rents them his honeymoon house? Sort of like a Native American Las Vegas? And he does P.I. work as his goodwill contribution?''

Ranger shrugged. ''How should I know? Anyway, Hannah, I think you're getting lost in the details. We're *married*. Not just in the eyes of God, but in the eyes of the law, as well.''

Hannah gasped. ''Married?''

He nodded, watching her carefully.

''Oh.'' Her gaze became strained.

''Yes, my little wife. How does that sound?''

''Well, it sounds—'' Hannah got up out of the bed, forgetting to limp. ''Well, it sounds…different,'' she said, edging toward the door. ''And I must say…it sounds different.''

He waited.

''You know,'' she said, ''I'm going to take a short walk and think about this, Ranger. A real short one. Just to take it all in. It's such a shock, you know. I'm speechless. Married. Won't everyone be so…surprised?''

And then she ran out the door.

''Amazing recovery, that,'' Ranger said. ''Mrs. Jefferson, I believe you just set a record for long-jumping that staircase.''

HANNAH RAN to the truck, telling herself not to hyperventilate. Married! He'd crept up on her with that one. "Breathe," she told herself. "Breathe!" She got behind the wheel and started the truck. She pressed the gas pedal so hard the engine revved like her heart.

And then she saw the letter on the seat next to her. In Ranger's handwriting.

Something told her it wasn't a love letter.

Hannah, I was pretty certain you wouldn't be happy when I told you that we are married. I know how upset you probably are, and the last thing I ever wanted to do was hurt you. I wouldn't want to be married to someone who doesn't want to be married to me. Rest assured that by the time you've broken the seal on this envelope, I've already called Brian and asked him to draw up divorce papers. Best of luck, and I hope you find the happiness that you're seeking.

Ranger

There was no one on the porch to watch her make her escape. She could go without anyone noticing. Ranger expected her to. He wanted her to. He understood how she was.

It didn't feel right.

Maybe she should walk back in the house and tell him not to start divorce proceedings. But she'd already lost Ranger. He would never be able to trust her. She could barely trust herself.

She didn't know what to do.

They'd hurt each other so many times.

Crying now, because it was all too painful and she didn't really understand why she couldn't be a woman who wanted a husband and a hearth and a home, she backed the truck up and headed toward Mississippi.

RANGER WATCHED from the upstairs window as Hannah ran to the truck. He saw her break open the letter. He called Brian. "Do it," was all he said, and Brian said, "Done." He hung up the phone, waiting as Hannah drove away, watching the truck disappear into the distance. As he had known it would.

She had done exactly as he'd expected her to. Which made him feel better about not telling her the truth.

That he'd fallen in love with her the minute he'd laid eyes on her red-tipped blond hair and cut-out tennis shoes. That he would have changed his life for her. That no one had taken hold of his heart the way she had.

He had not told her the truth, because it would not have made her happy to hear it. As Maverick had said, a man wanted what he couldn't have, and not always to his betterment.

"WHAT HAPPENED?" Jellyfish asked.

Hannah resolutely set out cards on the gaming table. The room was quiet because the customers hadn't yet ambled in from dinner. "Nothing happened. We were married, accidentally. We're getting divorced, on purpose.''

''But maybe you love him.''

She eyed her friend stoically. ''It doesn't matter. Ranger and I analyzed our relationship. We over-analyzed it, and under-analyzed it, and then we euthanised it. End of story.''

''Huh.'' Jellyfish rolled some dice toward the end of the table. ''So, what about Cissy?''

''I tried to call her today, but Valentine wouldn't put me through.'' Hannah cocked her head for a moment. ''Then she said the strangest thing; she wished Cissy had never come back because she's turned mean. Which is a truly spectacular thing for one of Marvella's girls to say, because they're not exactly short on that particular quality themselves.''

''I thought Cissy was nice.''

''Me, too. Sometimes a person acts a certain way when they're in a certain place as a defense mechanism.''

''You'd know all about that.''

Hannah gave Jellyfish a disgruntled eye. ''How so?''

''You act like a sister to me. When Ranger was around, you acted jumpy. Like he mattered, but you didn't want him to.''

''Well, when you and I decided to get married, we were doing it as a partnership. Neither you nor I believed in true love. It seemed like the smart thing to do.''

"And now?"

"And now I am married. And I would never again call a marriage of convenience a smart thing to do."

Jellyfish tossed the dice again, turning up snake eyes. "Maybe it wasn't so convenient."

"That's what we all know, now."

"I mean, maybe it was more a marriage of passion."

"Well, we definitely liked each other *that* way. But that's not love," Hannah said.

"Really? What is love?"

"Oh, I don't know, Jellyfish." Hannah sighed. "It's being there for each other. It's trusting each other. It's being breathless when you're eating oatmeal together."

"Maybe." He put the dice away and picked up a chip. "So. Hawk's picking up his truck from the pier, and you're coming with me."

"Right." She felt sad, and knew she'd feel sadder once the boat pulled away from shore, but fortunately she had Jellyfish, and he was really the only stable thing she'd ever had in her life.

Ranger had tried, though. If only she could have been more settled—

"I'm going to make a long-distance phone call before we go," she told Jellyfish.

"You've got thirty minutes. Take your time. I'm going to greet some tourists."

"Okay." In her room, she sat on her bed and put the phone in her lap. She stared at it a long time.

Then she pulled out a phone book she kept in the headboard cabinet and dialed the number.

"Hello?" a woman's voice said.

Hannah took a deep breath. "Mother, it's me. Hannah."

Chapter Seventeen

Mason stared out the window toward Mimi's house as rain fell in the darkness outside. "So, do you think Archer will call us eventually and let us know when he plans to return?"

Ranger wondered how much he should confess of his twin's plans. "I don't know."

Tex glanced over at him. "We're waiting for you to tell us where Hannah went, bro."

Another subject Ranger really didn't want to delve into. "I don't know."

"Don't know much, do you?" Last asked. "Or do you just not want to talk about anything?"

Ranger nodded, picking up his beer off the table. "That sums it up, I guess."

"Whatever happened to Cissy Kisserton?" Tex asked.

"I don't know," Ranger said.

"Well, that does it." Fannin sighed at the ceiling. "Don't ask him anything else. If Ranger says he doesn't know one more time, I'm going to whale him a good one.''

The rest of the brothers muttered their agreement.

''Is the sheriff going to make it?'' Ranger asked.

Mason sat down heavily on the sofa, flipping the channels on the muted TV. ''It's bad, that's all I know. I nearly had heart failure when I found the old man in bed like that. Dang, I thought he was already turning up daisies!'' He shook his head. ''I didn't know how the hell I was going to tell Mimi.''

Everyone digested this with sympathy. ''What are the chances of him getting a new liver?'' Bandera asked.

''Slim to none, probably,'' Mason answered.

''I wish I could do something,'' Navarro said.

''Look at that,'' Calhoun said. He pointed to the mute TV with his beer can. ''Doesn't your wife have a job on a riverboat, Ranger?''

''Turn it up, Mason,'' Crockett said.

The sound came on, and the announcer's voice accompanied pictures of a riverboat casino that had been rammed by another boat in Mississippi.

''That's Jellyfish's riverboat!'' Ranger exclaimed. His throat went dry and tight.

''Two died and there were several injuries—''

But Ranger didn't hear another word. He was already out the door, sure the Mississippi police could direct him to the right hospital.

The sight of the damaged riverboat had turned his stomach.

"EXCUSE ME," Ranger said to the intensive care nurse.

"Excuse me," he repeated. "I'd like to see Hannah Hotchkiss, please."

"I'm sorry. No one's admitted except family," the nurse replied.

"But she doesn't have any family here," Ranger told her. "Except Jellyfish. And I need to see him, too."

"I'm sorry, sir. No one is allowed in the ICU except family members."

A flash of inspiration hit. "Hannah's my wife."

The nurse raised a brow. "I'm sure she is. Why didn't you say that before, then?"

"I just remembered."

"I don't think so." The nurse prepared to turn away.

"Wait. Please."

She turned around.

"We got married by a medicine man. Here's our rings," he said, pulling the braided circles out of his wallet.

She frowned at him. "Sir, your story is not moving my heart to believe you." But she eyed the rings with interest. "Those are pretty unusual."

"But see, that's the deal. Hannah's an unusual woman. If you knew her, you'd understand that this is the kind of woman who would appreciate a ceremony in a Native American graveyard. She's not a conventional girl. She's afraid of things like commitment, and yet not afraid of snakes. She drinks beer and blows bubble gum. And the truth is, we're getting a divorce, or at least we're supposed to. But that's really because I need to pull my head out of my behind."

"Really?" the nurse said dryly.

"Yes. I've been trying to make her fit my memory of my parents' happy, normal marriage. That's never going to work for her. So I need to change the image."

"You love her, don't you?"

"I do. I really do," Ranger said. "I'm just sorry she had to capsize in the Mississippi for me to figure it out."

The nurse pursed her lips, undecided. "I'll have to ask her if she wants to see you, sir. What's your name?"

"Ranger Jefferson. I am so grateful to you. And if she says no, tell her…beg her."

"Don't push your luck, sir," the nurse told him. "Wait here."

WHEN THE NURSE returned thirty minutes later she said, "Miss Hotchkiss won't see you, Mr. Jefferson."

His heart sank. "Did she say why?"

The nurse dipped her head uncomfortably. "She said she doesn't need to be rescued."

"I see."

"I'm sorry." The nurse turned away to examine charts.

"Is Brother Jellyfish in ICU also?"

"Are you going to convince me that he, too, is a relation of yours?"

"It's this communal brotherhood thing," Ranger began. "We're all brothers on some level. You know, honey bees and snow-white turtledoves."

She didn't glance at him. "I can't give you any more information than I have."

He sighed. "All right. Thank you for trying. I'll be down here in case you need to find me. When my wife decides she wants to see me." Then Ranger stretched out on one of the vinyl chairs in the waiting room down the hall.

THREE DAYS LATER, Hannah still ached all over. Maybe what ached most was her heart, though. While it was thoughtful of Ranger to come visit her, she knew what had been wrong between them couldn't be changed.

At least not now. She didn't want him to see her hooked up to tubes, with bruises all over her face. She *looked* like she'd been in a shipwreck.

"How is Jellyfish today?" she asked the nurse.

"Getting ornery. We might be able to get him up for a short walk today."

Jellyfish had broken a few bones, including one in his foot and one in his wrist, when the other boat had crashed into theirs. Then he'd nearly drowned trying to rescue all the passengers who'd fallen in.

"A collapsed lung isn't fun," the nurse said. "But you're being a very good patient."

Hannah closed her eyes. "I want to complain. I just don't have the strength."

The nurse cleared her throat. "You know, that cowboy would probably love to pay you a visit."

She opened her eyes. "Ranger's still here? It's been three days."

"I know," the nurse said nonchalantly. "He says he's not leaving until he sees you and makes sure you're all right."

Hannah's eyes drifted closed. "I'm so sleepy."

"Go to sleep, then."

But the door opened, and a whirlwind of activity hit her room. Hannah tried to sit up. "Mother! Father!"

"Don't get up, Hannah. We're here to take care of our little girl," her mother said. "Nurse, you won't be needed anymore."

Hannah was too shocked to interrupt. The nurse didn't leave the room. She stared at the woman with the plaited gray hair to her waist and the bald-headed man with the moustache nearly as long as his companion's hair.

"Excuse me," the nurse interjected. "This patient needs rest."

"This patient needs prayer," Hannah's mother said. "And a lot of it, from what I can see. Hannah, honey, we'll have you out of here as soon as possible."

It was her nightmare all over again. "Mother," Hannah said weakly, "this is the Intensive Care Unit. I can't just go home."

"She's not going anywhere," the nurse agreed. "You, however, must abide by standard visiting hours."

"You can't stop us from praying," Hannah's father said. "We believe in the power of prayer and holistic medicine, *not* the power of doctors and hospitals."

"Your daughter could have died," the nurse snapped. "Now please leave before I call security."

"We'll be speaking to your supervisor," Hannah's mother said ominously as they exited.

"I'm so sorry," the nurse said. "Can I get you anything?"

"No, thank you." Hannah could barely mumble. She was so tired and she felt so ill, and now that she'd seen her parents, she was distressed. Suddenly she was again a teenager, desperately ill and needing doctors and an operation.

It was Jellyfish who'd convinced his father to slip her into the city to see a physician and then specialists. They'd taken her to the hospital for the operation. Jellyfish's family paid the bills.

Many years later, when Jellyfish left the commune and purchased the riverboat, Hannah repaid the debt by working for him six months out of every year. It was a bond between them that stayed strong.

But she'd been on the phone with her mother, trying to salvage something from her painful past, when the riverboat got rammed. Her mother had heard her scream and had come here to make certain Hannah was cared for properly.

No, not properly. Cared for on *her* terms.

Her parents still didn't get it.

But now she did.

"Nurse, there is something you could get me," she said, her voice barely a whisper. "That handsome cowboy down the hall? Please tell him I need him."

"GUESS WHAT, cowboy?"

Ranger opened his eyes to see the nurse looking down at him with a smile.

"She wants to see you."

He jumped to his feet. "What changed her mind? Is she okay?"

The nurse laughed. "I think I'll let her tell you."

Ranger tore down the hall and into Hannah's room, holding back the gasp when he saw her face. "Oh, Hannah. Oh, boy. You look like you've been in a barroom brawl with the Jefferson boys."

"Oh, God, don't make me laugh," Hannah said, managing a smile. "It hurts way too much."

"I won't even tell the smallest joke. Um, the nurse said you wanted to see me?"

"I need a rescue, if you've got one left in you."

"Whew. I never thought I'd hear those words come from your lips! Are you sure you didn't crack your skull?"

"You said you wouldn't make me laugh." Hannah groaned. "And I'm about to."

"Don't do that! I don't want to be sent out of here by the sentry."

"The what?"

"The nurse. She guards you like a hound guards his dinner!"

Hannah nodded. "I know. She's been wonderful. They don't pay her enough, I'm sure."

"Hey!" Ranger said. "What'd you need from me, then?"

"First," Hannah said, "I want you to find Jellyfish and check on him. I get a periodic update from my nurse, but he's on a different floor, so it's an effort for her. I want you to lay eyes on him and make certain he doesn't need anything."

Ranger tried not to be jealous that the first thing Hannah asked for was a Jellyfish report. "And then?"

"And then I really need you to be married to me."

He couldn't help it; his jaw dropped. "Married?"

"Yes. Mother's here, and she's determined to rescue me. Only her rescuing nearly ruined my life. Could we be married just a few more days, at least until she returns to the commune?"

"I don't know if it'll work," Ranger said. "The nurse is suspicious of the depth of our commitment."

"It won't be a problem," Hannah assured him.

"I don't get it."

"As a husband, you'll have rights my parents can't override. You'll be my next-of-kin, as it were. My guardian. My lawful protection. But just until I'm out of the hospital.''

''Oh, Hannah,'' Ranger said with a grin as he slipped her braided ring back on her finger, ''You have no idea how much I'm going to enjoy this charade.''

Chapter Eighteen

"You can't keep us from our daughter," Hannah heard her mother say in the hallway.

"Five minutes," the nurse said sternly.

"Oh, no," Hannah moaned.

Ranger patted her hand. "Don't worry. I've got it covered. You just lie there and look pretty."

Her mother and father stopped when they saw Ranger's bulk next to their daughter. "Who are you?"

He stood, his hand out. "I'm Ranger Jefferson, Hannah's husband. Pleased to meet you."

"Husband?" her mother repeated. "Husband? As in married?"

"Yes," Ranger said cheerfully. He held up his hand and Hannah's. "With matching rings even."

Her mother stared for a moment. "Rope? Very economical."

"Well, you know Hannah's not a girl for pretensions," he said. "Are you, muffin?"

Hannah pressed her lips together so she wouldn't

laugh, but later, she was going to show Ranger just what marriage to a muffin entailed. "No pretensions here."

Her mother blinked, neither pleased nor convinced. Her father hung in the background, seemingly speechless. "Why didn't we know about this?" her mother asked.

"She was going to tell you. That's why she called. I kind of swept her off her feet," Ranger said, making it up as he went along. "And truthfully, *I* got swept so hard I nearly rolled away. In fact, I still find an occasional grain of sand in my ears."

Hannah cleared her throat to warn him that enough was enough. He grinned at her.

"I'm not sure if I believe this," her mother said, her tone displeased. "Hannah has a tendency to…twist the facts when she's being stubborn."

"Oh, Hannah doesn't lie," Ranger assured her. "Hannah obfuscates, maybe, but she never lies."

"That will be enough, husband," Hannah said through her teeth.

He patted her hand. "We're ever so happy together. We were meant to be. Like two peas in a pod. Two ribbons in a little girl's hair."

"Ranger!" Hannah said.

"I cannot imagine you married to this man," her mother said. "He seems…odd."

"Well, nevertheless," Ranger said, kissing the tips of Hannah's fingers, "this is my little sugarcake, and as soon as she's well, I'm taking her out of here."

"We were planning to secure her release today. She'd get well much faster with us."

"Excuse me, I didn't get your names?" Ranger said. "Rude of me, I know, but I can be slow on details."

"I'm Pandora, and this is Planet Hotchkiss."

"You don't say," Ranger said dryly. "Again, it's a treat to meet you. Well, having spoken to the nurse, who is quite capable, and having consulted the physician, we feel it is in Hannah's best interests to have a conventional medical path to wellness at this time."

"Another obfuscation, my studmuffin?" Hannah murmured under her breath.

He patted her hand.

"Well, we feel, as her parents, that we have a better knowledge of—"

"Mother," Hannah said sternly. "I trust my husband to make the right decisions for me. And I trust myself even more. I called you so that we could put the past behind us. But if you're going to try to force your way of life on me, you might as well go back home." She took a deep breath. "Only if you do, it's the last time I'm going to be the one to make the phone call."

Pandora took a step back. "Your tone is disrespectful."

"My tone is honest. Take it or leave it, Mother. Father. I'm finished running through life afraid I can't trust anyone to truly want what's best for me. I don't need to do it anymore." She felt Ranger squeeze her hand and was glad he was there. "I trust myself to make my own decisions, my own mistakes and, most of all, my own happiness."

AFTER Hannah's parents left, looking like a couple of naturally squeezed oranges, Ranger kissed his wife on the forehead. "I guess you're worn out from that."

She looked at him, and his heart expanded inside him. But he knew better than to hope. She'd just told her parents how she felt about them trying to change her. He sure wasn't going to make the mistake they had.

"I am worn out," she said, "but not by you. Thank you for being there for me."

"You mean, I pulled off a decent rescue?" he teased.

"Shut up and sit back down." She patted the bed beside her. "In fact, as soon as they pull this tube out of me, I may want to try out this hospital bed. With you."

That sounded like a maneuver Ranger could manage. "I am always happy to be of service."

She gazed at him. "Why didn't you leave? Why did you hang around for three days?"

"Because you needed me, even if you didn't know it. And I love you." Now he was stepping into the danger zone, Ranger knew. If there was ever a time for him to get the boot, it was now. He held his breath.

She nodded at him. "I'm in love with you, too."

"For how long?"

"It started at the rodeo last month. The feeling built when you picked me and Cissy up. It hit last-forever when you put the letter about divorce in the truck. That's when I knew you understood me better than I understood myself. And I like it," she told him. "I've never had anyone accept me for myself. Warts, bumps, bruises and all."

"Jellyfish?" Ranger asked, forcing down his jealousy.

"Is a friend. We could never marry each other for real. Not the way I want it to be with you. Do you know you haven't mentioned that stupid curse once since you've been in the hospital?"

"That's because it turned out to be the Curse of the Drunken Boat Driver," Ranger said. "Anyway, I don't believe in curses anymore. True love has cured me of that."

They gazed at each other. "What about your military aspirations?" Hannah asked.

"Maybe my military aspiration is to give you a nine-gun salute every morning."

She nodded. "That sounds promising. But where will we live?"

"Not on that damn riverboat, that's for sure," Ranger said. "I need something solid under my feet. How about my truck? Or even an RV? We'll just keep moving on."

She giggled. "So, we're going to be vagabonds together."

"I like seeing the country and doing new things. You fit in my truck okay. You survive on beef jerky and soda like a real woman. What else do I need?"

She glowed, and he fell even more in love. "Hannah, will you marry me? For real, this time? In a church, with the family present, and a minister? I like Hawk and all, but I'm not certain his ceremony had the proper stick-it power. And I definitely want this marriage to stick."

"If you can handle an unorthodox way of life, Ranger, then my answer is yes. Absolutely yes!"

"As far as I can see, we'll both have all the excitement we can manage. And I call that a good thing." Ranger took Hannah in his arms and kissed her long and slow, though gently because of the tubes. They embraced, relaxing in nothing more than the feel of each other. And then he put his face in her hair. "I will love going nowhere with you."

Because somehow, nowhere with Hannah felt like the perfect destination.

Epilogue

The wedding was a romantic riverboat affair. Evening stars glowed as Hannah and Ranger said their marriage vows. Jellyfish gave the barefoot bride away, though bare feet were the only non-traditional part of Hannah's ensemble. Her stylist sisters had found her a lovely gown and veil, and even managed to talk Ranger into a tux.

The newly repaired riverboat was festooned with tiny white lights and gardenias—everyone agreed it was the perfect place to hold a wedding. Both branches of Delilah's salon had come to see their sister married, and the girls did a wonderful job of keeping the Jefferson brothers, Jellyfish and Hawk from being bored. They simply flirted the evening away, and gambled, and there might have even been a playfully stolen kiss or two.

"Since Marvella passed on the cowboy raffle idea, we should use it," Jessica said, gazing with longing at all the handsome men.

"I agree," said Kiki. "Think of the money we could raise."

"It would be the first thing the two salons have gotten to do together," Shasta pointed out. "Union Junction and Lonely Hearts together again."

"We'd have to think of a good cause," Gretchen said.

"Sticking it to Marvella is good enough for me." Velvet dipped into the punch bowl and served her sisters as they clustered around.

"Raising money for charity is good enough for me," Jessica said. "We could do it at the next rodeo. It would be such a novel idea, I'm sure we'd draw a huge audience. What woman wouldn't want to bid on gorgeous men?"

Gretchen shook her head. "If we can talk all these guys into doing it. What's the motivation for them?"

"Free haircuts," Remy suggested.

"They rarely get a haircut, and it's just a little trim on the ends when they do," Violet stated. Then she snapped her fingers. "Homecooked meals for a week!"

"Taken to their house," Tisha said, warming to the idea.

"No fair," someone complained. "That means only the girls in Union Junction get to participate. We're too far away to take food to them."

"Well," Gretchen said, thinking hard, "Then you girls offer to come out and clean out the barns for them one weekend. Or some other chore that requires their full attention. You can be their personal slaves for a day.''

''I like that idea,'' Kiki said.

They looked at the cowboys, who were grouped around the gambling table.

''It may become more of a cowboy hunt than a raffle,'' Shasta said, ''but we won't tell them that.''

''Oh, no,'' Gretchen agreed. ''What they don't know certainly can't scare them!''

''I'm ready to have rice thrown on me,'' Lily said. The women's attention turned to the newlyweds. Across the room, Ranger and Hannah danced together, close and intimate. ''They make a beautiful couple,'' Lily said on a sigh.

Hannah smiled, knowing she'd never dreamed she could be so happy. Marrying Ranger made her life complete. To her relief, her parents had decided to skip the occasion. Too much time had passed between Hannah's childhood and Hannah's adult years, and though they agreed to keep in touch occasionally, Hannah knew that the rest of her life would be devoted to Ranger.

''From arroyo to riverboat,'' Ranger said to his bride. ''You'll never be able to say that I kept you in a pumpkin shell.''

''And you'll never be able to say that I tied you down,'' Hannah teased. ''It's kind of fun being footloose and fancy-free, isn't it?''

''As long as my finger's tied, I'm happy.'' And it was true. Ranger knew he was going to love the ups and downs of being married to Hannah. They'd had gold rings made that matched the rope rings they'd originally married with, but he still wore his rope ring, too. For good luck. He was, after all, a somewhat superstitious man. "So, how about another chance to kiss the bride, *Mrs.* HotKiss?"

She laughed as she slid her arms around his neck. "You really can't call me that anymore."

He took her wrists as she slid them behind his neck so that he could pull her tighter against him. "Oh, yes, I can."

And then he proved it.

Turn the page for a sneak preview of
TEX TIMES TEN (AR #989),
the next book in Tina Leonard's miniseries
COWBOYS BY THE DOZEN.
Available October 2003!

Chapter One

Tex Jefferson didn't have the desire to avoid matrimony that his brothers, Frisco Joe, Laredo and Ranger had possessed. It was as if his brothers had tried so hard to outrun the matrimonial state that they'd swerved and crashed headfirst into it.

Tex simply wasn't going to be caught like that. Running was not a fail-safe cure. His brothers had married good women, and they were happy changing their worlds to suit their new wives. Ranger had even married Hannah twice—once on this very riverboat.

But I, Tex thought, *know that stability is not my thing.* He could ride the orneriest bull. He could bust heads when defense was necessary and sometimes when it wasn't. Rope, ride, range.

But he would die coming home to an Annabelle, a Katy or even a Hannah every night. Though they were good girls, every one of them. And Tex was happy for his brothers.

Now Mimi Cannady, their next-door-neighbor, had put a knot in his eldest brother, Mason's life. Merry hellfire was Mimi. Tex thought he could almost handle a woman like that.

Maybe. If forced.

But why should he fall for a lady whom he had no intention of marrying? Mason hadn't married Mimi, and surely that was an example to be followed!

Shoving away the thought that Mason was miserable, Tex wandered into one of the riverboat's many bedrooms. He couldn't see himself living on a boat the way Jellyfish did. Too confining. Too narrow. Rivers had their charm but nothing like the great open spaces of Texas.

Startled, he realized he'd stumbled into the newly decorated honeymoon suite—Hannah's bedroom converted for that purpose, as Ranger had mentioned. There were white roses galore and two crystal flutes on the nightstand. Fascinated, Tex ogled the place where love ended up. You met a girl, you married a girl and then you bedded down with the girl, every night for the rest of your life.

Sheesh. Not me, Tex thought.

Next to the crystal flutes was a book that bore Hannah Hotchkiss's name. She'd be Hannah Jefferson now. Through the window, he could still hear the sound of dance music and happy guests on deck.

He was forgoing dancing for snooping. But he had thought Cissy Kisserton might make it to Hannah's wedding, since the two of them had gotten close during their infamous road trip with Ranger. He'd hoped for a glimpse of that silver-haired man-magnet. Whew. A glimpse was about all a man could handle.

Being nosy, Tex picked up the book. A picture fell to the floor, which he scooped up guiltily.

And there was Cissy Kisserton, looking like no Cissy he'd ever seen. She wasn't dressed in a mini-skirt and high heels. She wasn't wreaking havoc on a man's groin by wearing catsuit jeans.

This Cissy was dressed for church.

Whew. She was a wicked brew of sin underneath that churchy lace thing. Who was she trying to fool?

Tex wasn't admitting it, but he'd stayed on that bull, Bad Ass Blue, just to impress Cissy. Sure she'd lied about the other bull, Bloodthirsty, pulling left so that Tex's twin, Laredo, wouldn't be able to stay on.

But Tex sort of admired a woman with gall.

And he'd stayed on his bull just to show Cissy Kisserton what he was made of. He figured she'd be appropriately admiring and grateful after the rodeo.

She hadn't been.

It was as if she had too many things on her mind to be bothered with him. A winning cowboy, and she hadn't given him the time of day. He'd beat his own brother—not that it was difficult since Laredo couldn't have stayed on a bull if he'd had Krazy Glue on his jeans—just to get *her* attention.

Tex turned his gaze back to the picture. There were seven moppets standing around Cissy. The church was in the background. In fact, she was standing in the church parking lot! A baby stroller at her side held what looked like two infants and, he saw with a growing sort of horror, her left hand was on the stroller handle!

Tex's jaw sagged as if he'd been punched in a bar brawl. The nine little moppets of varying ages were going to church with *her*.

Coming soon from

AMERICAN *Romance*®

Cowboys
BY
THE DOZEN!

by

TINA LEONARD

The Jefferson brothers of Malfunction Junction,
Texas, know how to lasso a lady's heart—
and then let it go without a ruckus.

But these twelve rowdy ranchers are in for the
ride of their lives when the local ladies begin
rounding up hearts and domesticating
cowboys...by the dozen.

Don't miss—
FRISCO JOE'S FIANCÉE (HAR #977)
available 7/03

LAREDO'S SASSY SWEETHEART (HAR #981)
available 8/03

RANGER'S WILD WOMAN (HAR #986)
available 9/03

TEX TIMES TEN (HAR #989)
available 10/03

Available at your favorite retail outlet.
Only from Harlequin Books!

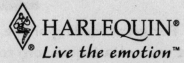

HARLEQUIN®
Live the emotion™

Visit us at www.americanromances.com

Forrester Square

LEGACIES · LIES · LOVE ·

July 19, 1983...

The Kinards, the Richardses and the Webbers—Seattle's
Kennedys. Their "compound"—elegant Forrester Square...
until the fateful night that tore these families apart.

Twenty years later...

Their children were reunited. Repressed memories and
family secrets were about to be revealed. And one person
was out to make sure they never remembered...

Save $1.00 off

your purchase of any
Harlequin® Forrester Square title
on-sale August 2003 through July 2004

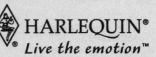

Forrester Square

LEGACIES . LIES . LOVE .

July 19, 1983...

The Kinards, the Richardses and the Webbers—Seattle's Kennedys. Their "compound"—elegant Forrester Square... until the fateful night that tore these families apart.

Twenty years later...

Their children were reunited. Repressed memories and family secrets were about to be revealed. And one person was out to make sure they never remembered...

Save $1.00 off

your purchase of any
Harlequin® Forrester Square title
on-sale August 2003 through July 2004

RETAILER: Harlequin Enterprises Ltd. will pay the face value of this coupon plus 10.25¢ if submitted by customer for this product only. Any other use constitutes fraud. Coupon is nonassignable. Void if taxed, prohibited or restricted by law. Void if copied. Consumer must pay any government taxes. Valid in Canada only. Nielson Clearing House customers—mail to: Harlequin Enterprises Ltd., 661 Millidge Avenue, P.O. Box 639, Saint John, N.B. E2L 4A5. Non NCH retailer—for reimbursement submit coupons and proof of sales directly to: Harlequin Enterprises Ltd., Retail Sales Dept., 225 Duncan Mill Rd., Don Mills, Ontario M3B 3K9, Canada.

Coupon expires July 30, 2004.
Redeemable at participating retail outlets in Canada only.
Limit one coupon per purchase.

52605231

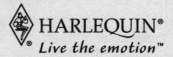

HARLEQUIN®
Live the emotion™

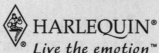

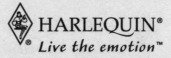